ON TOUR

the backup singer

*What is
the color of
friendship?*

barb huff

BARBOUR
PUBLISHING

dedication

For Mistey, Julie, Mr. DiDonato,
and, of course, my husband Frank,
for being the ones who most believed
that this was all possible.

And special thanks to
my brother, David Keffer,
for sharing the lyrics to his songs.

about the author

Barb Huff is a former director of youth and family programs. She has published devotionals on parenting and teen nonfiction articles in *Guideposts for Teens, Group,* and other publications. She lives in northeastern Ohio with her husband, son, and foster children.

CHAPTER 11

"Are you even black?"

Shanice Stevenson dragged her heel on the sidewalk, bringing her in-line skates to a halt. With a flick of her ankles, she spun herself around to face the girl who had spoken to her with such malice.

The two teenaged boys accompanying her also skidded to a stop and turned toward the unfamiliar voice.

Elijah Greer, the taller of the two boys, skated over and took his friend by the arm. "Come on, 'Nice," he said gingerly, using her pet name and trying to diffuse the situation. "We aren't looking for any trouble. Let's skate."

The newcomer stood in the middle of the sidewalk, hands perched on her hips. Her eyes were fixed steadily on Shanice, challenging her to give an answer. The girl appeared to be in her mid-teens like the trio before her, but she wasn't a familiar face in their tight-knit neighborhood.

Chill, 'Nice, chill. Don't be stupid and don't give her the satisfaction. Just get away from her. Yeah, easier said than done.

The other boy, Parker Blevins, looked uneasily from one girl to the other. Shanice knew that look—he wasn't really afraid of what she might do, but he was going to stay close to her, acting overprotective as usual. Their friendship went a long way back; he had a way of always looking out for her.

"Nah, 'Lijah," she replied, "I'm good."

The other girl shifted her weight from one hip to the other in an exaggerated show of impatience. Her tight, spiraled curls bounced with her, lightly brushing in front of her eyes. Lifting a perfectly manicured hand to swipe the hair from her face, she sneered at Shanice. The white and Carolina blue colors in her Sean John shirt and matching basketball pants highlighted her almond-shaped eyes and dark skin perfectly.

Shanice shuffled her feet a bit within her well-worn black in-line skates. Stuffing her hands in the pockets of the army-green pants that hung loosely from her own thin waist, she returned the smug smile. Shanice Stevenson was not one to back down from a challenge.

"Come on, Shanice," Parker pleaded. "Let's just roll. This isn't worth the trouble."

Suddenly, Shanice rolled her eyes and released a "psh" from her lips, flipping her palm toward the girl as she turned toward the boys. "Let's go. You're right, Parker. It's not worth it. That's only my cousin Tawny."

The boys scrambled after her as she skated down the street.

"I didn't know you had any cousins around here," Parker said cautiously. The handsome fifteen year old wore baggy wide-leg jeans, a form-fitting white T-shirt, and a black stocking cap over his sandy-blond curls.

"She's staying with us for awhile, I guess. Tawny and her brother too. I don't know, I just live there," she said dismissively, making it clear she hadn't had a choice in the matter.

Hurrying toward the curb, Shanice jumped on the sidewalk and slid her skates along its edge in perfect front-grind form.

Now you're just showing off....

She had to smile at herself as she hopped off the curb and skated in a circle. Tawny had once been as close as a sister to her. In their younger days, the two fifteen year olds would spend hours in Shanice's room dancing and belting out their favorite songs. They'd stay up long after dark flipping through hip-hop magazines and daydreaming over the artists.

Once upon a time, Shanice would count down the days on her calendar until summertime when Tawny would come to stay with them for a few weeks. But Shanice had outgrown all that kid stuff. And the last time they spent time together, it was evident to her that her cousin had not. Shanice had turned into an individual, and Tawny seemed to be a walking MTV commercial. Shanice was fairly sure they had nothing left in common.

This is going to be a long, awkward summer for me.

This summer Tawny was staying indefinitely. Add the fact that her two-year-old brother was coming as well, and for the first time. Shanice was not looking forward to the next three months.

Pulling the red clip out of her hair, Shanice noticed her mother standing in the front door of their home. Shanice shook her head lightly, allowing the multitude of tight, tiny braids to cascade down her neck. Even though at times she was proud of her shoulder-length locks, she easily found her hair annoying when it wasn't braided and out of her face.

Now I'm busted.

JaNay Stevenson did not take bad manners lightly. Her only daughter would be in serious trouble if she were being impolite to anyone— even if the person deserved it. And Shanice had been picked on before about her skin color. She was too dark to be called "white" but too light to be "black." Mama would never accept that reality as a viable reason to be coarse with anyone. . .especially a member of the family.

Thankfully, the teasing came in short spurts, usually from her cousins when they would get together. Once, ten-year-old Shanice had run to her mother and buried her face into Mama's thin frame at a family reunion as she cried over the words of an older cousin on the playground.

"You can't fight ignorance with tears," her mother had told her. "Dry those eyes, sweets, and go show him that it's not the wrapper but what's on the inside that makes a person."

Mama needs to have that talk with Tawny.

"Come on, guys," she mumbled dejectedly to the boys. They followed her as she skated back toward her cousin. "Hey, Tawny," she said dutifully as she drew close.

Mama, seemingly satisfied, disappeared from the door.

Her cousin crossed her arms in front of her chest, poised for a battle of words. Shanice wasn't even going there—she knew she had little chance to win against the quick-witted teen. She'd found out that fact the hard way in the past.

"Some friends of mine I want you to meet," Shanice continued. "This is Parker and Elijah." She pointed to each respectively, and they smiled and nodded cordially.

"Um, yeah," Tawny replied, rolling her eyes again. "Aunt 'Nay said you need to come back to the house and help get our stuff upstairs."

Man, get your own stuff upstairs!

Passing pointedly by the stack of suitcases and boxes sitting in the driveway, Tawny turned and walked back toward the house.

No, no, no. This is not what the summer is going to be all about! I'm not waiting on your sorry face this whole time.

"Well, grab something," Shanice retorted, pulling off her skates.

Tawny kept walking. "I need to find Jalin," she replied.

"Well, you can do it with one of your bags in your hand. Don't think I'm carrying this all up there by myself."

Opening the screen door into the kitchen, Tawny glanced over her shoulder and smugly replied, "Put your little boyfriends to use then."

Mama!" Shanice belted out as she followed Tawny into the house. The screen door banged shut behind her, rattling the row of terra cotta pots planted with herbs that sat on a wooden stepladder.

JaNay Stevenson appeared through the dining room entryway with a dust cloth in hand. The strong smell of lemon-scented cleaner followed her.

Tawny trailed along behind Shanice with her brother held close to her chest. The curly-headed little boy squirmed as if he wanted down, but she held tight. His arm was tangled in his overall straps, and he whined as he tried to free himself. His sister paid no attention.

"How many times have I told you not to let the screen door close like that?" her mother asked in a soft, firm, but patient voice. Her tiny athletic frame was an inch or so shorter than her only child's, but her poise made her gigantic. Her thick black hair was straightened into a professional, shoulder-length style that framed her oval face, and even though she was cleaning house, her makeup was picture perfect.

"Mama," Shanice began to plead her case, "she. . ."

"Close the door the right way, please."

Parker stood in the doorway, unsure if he should come in or head home. He eased the old country-style wooden door closed, the heavy spring groaning in opposition to its slow motion. Elijah was still outside, pretending to fiddle with the straps on his skates. It was obvious he wanted nothing to do with the lecture about to go down inside.

9

Looking at her cousin and then her mother, Shanice tried again. "She needs to. . ."

"You," her mother interrupted, "need to close that door the right way."

Shanice dramatically circled around the white-tiled kitchen table in the middle of the room and pushed open the door with one hand. The spring once again groaned as she rolled her eyes at her friend still outside and closed it slowly.

This is so humiliating. Why does she have to treat me like I'm five in front of my friends? And if Tawny doesn't get that grin off her face. . .

Elijah raised an eyebrow and shrugged in return; he was not going to be involved in this battle. JaNay Stevenson had been his eighth-grade Sunday school teacher, and he had learned quickly not to cross her willingly.

"If you'll excuse me, I have some cleaning to get to. Now," her mother continued, "if you have a situation that needs solving, then I do believe you need to talk to that person and work it out instead of bellowing at me."

That's where the problem lies. I don't even want to speak to her. We shouldn't even have to have this conversation.

Shanice had no interest in talking anything out—her cousin needed to get herself outside and get her stuff up to her room. Tawny had nothing wrong with her that she couldn't pick up a suitcase or two, and her rudeness had lost her the chance of having some willing help now. Shanice was willing to share her house and her parents with Tawny for a few months, but she was not going to stand by and be reduced to the role of maid in her own home.

Shanice scowled at Tawny again. That girl was lucky she was spending the summer with them instead of Grandma Leona. At least here she might get to see another teen or two instead of spending the summer picking and snapping beans out of Grandma's garden. Shanice loved her grandma, but a whole summer with her would have to be the longest time of one's life.

Taking the squirming toddler from his sister's arms, Shanice's mom shot her daughter a firm look and headed toward the living room.

"You getting my stuff?" Tawny asked, her voice dripping with glee over the events that had transpired. "You can just take it up to my room. It was a long flight and I think I might just chill on the couch and watch some videos or something. I'm exhausted."

With an exasperated sigh, Shanice grabbed Parker by the arm and pulled him through the door and toward the driveway. The creaking porch door started to swing shut, but Parker caught it and closed it gently.

"Let's go," Shanice demanded.

"Where we going?" Parker asked, slipping his feet back into his skates.

Shanice shrugged as she snapped the closures on her pair and got to her feet. "Anywhere but here."

"Your ma's going to kill you," Elijah said while looking nervously back toward the house. JaNay Stevenson was nowhere in sight. Neither was Tawny. "Maybe we should just get this stuff in the house?"

Heading toward the street, Shanice called back, "Don't even touch it. Gotta take a stand sometimes, dawg. Let's go."

If I carry her stuff in all by myself, I'll be waiting on her hand and foot all summer. There's nothing wrong with her—no reason she can't at least help a little bit. So her parents are getting divorced? Like no one saw that coming. But how come Mama doesn't see it? I am so dead when I get back.

She hopped over a manhole cover and turned in the air, landing so she could face her home. Her cousin stepped into view through a front window of the gray century-old farmhouse. Shanice turned away and started after the boys down the road. Something inside nagged at her as she pulled away from the boys, skating as fast as she could down the empty side street. Tawny's face had shown no more signs of malice— she had even looked a bit sad.

Not my problem. It's the principle of the thing.

CHAPTER 33

Closing the door gently behind her, Shanice crept into the darkened kitchen. She could hear the TV in the living room. The tangy smell of oven-baked barbecue aroused her senses as she placed her skates in the basket beside the door.

Oh man, she was hungry. Hopefully it was pulled pork over homemade bread—her mama's specialty. And wherever there was pulled pork with homemade bread, corn on the cob and home-fried potatoes were on the side. She must still have something in common with her cousin: their favorite meal.

I can see it now. We'll spend the summer talking about corn on the cob and learning the proper techniques for baking bread.

Yeah, right.

She smiled at herself. Mama would probably be giddy over the idea.

The last of the day's sun peeked through the windows overlooking the backyard, casting shadows across the clean countertops. Shanice had missed dinner. She was really in trouble now. Mama's one rule was that you always had to be home by dinner, and never before had Shanice disobeyed it. Opening the refrigerator, she scoured around for a plate saved for her. In seventh grade, when she played volleyball one season, Mama had made up a plate, covered it with foil, and left it on the top shelf for her to eat after every game.

This time there wasn't any plate. All the leftovers were stored away in containers.

Shanice looked through the doorway into the living room. Mama was building a block tower with Jalin on the floor. Tawny was sprawled over the couch, probably in the same place she said she was going to be when Shanice left, and her dad sat in his chair reading the paper. No one seemed to notice that she was home.

As she walked over to the cupboard, she heard footsteps on the foyer's hardwood floor.

Mama was coming.

Just play it cool. No big deal. Play it cool.

Folding her arms, Mama leaned against the doorframe. Pretending she didn't see her there, Shanice placed her plate on the table and went to the refrigerator. She scooped up the pulled pork and corn containers and went about making her plate. Mama watched with her arms still pulled tight across her chest and her lips pursed in thought. Then she reached into the refrigerator and retrieved a container of fried apples and a pitcher of iced tea.

"There were no potatoes left," she stated, as if that were an explanation for it all. "I'll make you some if you'd like." She put ice in two glasses and placed them on the table.

Shanice shook her head and stuffed her plate in the microwave. Pouring them both some tea, Mama took a seat at the table.

They sat down together as Shanice prayed over her meal and began to eat.

Mama ran her finger around the top of her glass of iced tea as she watched her daughter. Finally she spoke. "You want to tell me what started this whole thing?"

"Not particularly," Shanice replied. She knew what Mama would say—that she needed to stop being so sensitive to her cousin's teasing and just "be herself." The problem was, "herself" was what Tawny obviously didn't like anymore.

Mama took a sip of her tea, the ice clinking as she swirled it slightly.

"I know this is going to be an adjustment."

"No, Mama," said Shanice. "It's fine. We'll just keep our distance from each other or something."

There was nothing worse than hearing that little hint of disappointment in her mom's voice. Shanice was willing to agree to just about anything to hear Mama change her tone. She hated to disappoint her mother.

"Tonya is at a rough age right now, and she doesn't have the kind of support you do to make it through this time in her life. And with all this stuff with her parents compounding things, it's a wonder she's not a total wreck. She's still trying to decide if she wants to be 'Tonya' or 'Tawny,' the little kid. It's going to be an adjustment for all of us over the next few months." She paused as she took a drink of her tea, visibly contemplating what to say next. "But they need support, and my sister needs us to care for her children right now. Family is family, Shanice. They're the ones who'll always be there for you."

Shanice nodded while playing with the apples on her plate. She didn't completely believe in the whole family-being-the-only-ones-who'll-always-be-there-for-you stuff. Other than her parents, she wasn't close to any of her family members, though she did love Grandma Leona. Grandma was the only one who didn't look at her and see "half-white" written across her forehead. It would be stretching the truth to say that she even liked any of the rest of them that well. They sure didn't seem to be there for her family very often.

The voracious appetite that had followed her in had slipped back out the door. Even the pulled pork dripping in honey barbecue sauce had lost its flavor.

"There's one thing you need to know, young lady. From this moment on," her mother's voice grew stern, "you will not eat dinner if you are not at the table here when I put the food out. I am not playing this game all summer. This is not how things are done in my house. You eat with us or you are responsible for feeding yourself, and that does not include helping yourself to my leftovers when you get back."

Again, Shanice nodded.

Mama's voice softened again as she finished the last of her tea and leaned across the table toward her daughter. "Now I'd like to see you patch things over with your cousin. I'm not going to have two teenage girls at each other's throats all summer long, you understand?"

Jalin bounded into the room and tackled his aunt with a big laugh. He looked up at Shanice with his head still resting on his aunt's lap. Shanice smiled at him and realized that he had the same almond-shaped dark eyes as her mom; his eyes matched her mama's perfectly.

"Hi," he said.

"Hello," Shanice replied. She was having a hard time with the similarities between the two year old and her mother. They even had the same milky dark skin tone and small, slightly rounded nose.

My cousins look more like my mother than I do. Weird.

The pit of her stomach tingled at the thought. Excusing herself, Shanice cleaned her plate and utensils and went into the living room.

Her father smiled at her and turned his head as she entered the room so she could peck him on the cheek. The knot in his tie was pulled loosely to the side to allow the top button of his shirt to be open, and the newspaper lay across his khaki slacks. Shanice had his round, quizzical eyes, though his were green and hers a hazel brown. Sitting on the arm of his chair, she kissed him on the cheek like she had done nearly every evening for as long as she could remember.

"How's my girl?" he asked as he turned down the sound on the television. Shanice briefly caught a glimpse of her cousin's disgust—probably at the fact that she couldn't hear the program anymore. "Where have you been?" he queried.

"Out with some boys," Tawny piped in.

Shanice shot her a dirty look. Not like what she said mattered. Her dad knew whom she was with before she even replied. "I was out skating and stuff with 'Lijah and Parker."

"Nice night for it," he replied. "Did you get some good shred time?"

"Whatever, Dad," she laughed. "You're just so ancient."

"We called it 'shredding' in my day." He laughed with her. "Back when we had to skate barefoot in the snow uphill both ways. We had to fashion the wheels ourselves out of rocks."

"You're so weird, Dad," she dismissed him with an exaggerated roll of the eyes.

Yeah, just try to get me in trouble with my daddy. You'll lose that one for sure.

Cocking her head, Shanice smiled dryly at her cousin. Much to her surprise, Tawny flashed a real smile back.

Okay, what was that about? Maybe the old Tawny's back?

Puzzled, she diverted her attention to Jalin and Mama as they returned to the floor and their block building. Mama giggled as the two-year-old karate kicked the tower, sending pieces flying all over the floor. Her dad scrambled to help pick them up. As he stood up, he bopped Tawny on the head with his newspaper and smiled at her.

"Well," Shanice stated, feeling a bit awkward in her own living room, "I need a shower. In case anyone notices I'm gone."

No one acknowledged her as she made her way to the stairs.

I will be a stranger in my own house the whole summer.

Tawny and Jalin's suitcases and boxes blocked the staircase. The larger boxes sat in the hallway while the suitcases took up the bottom two stairs. It seemed like a lot of stuff to Shanice for only a few months' stay.

She kicked a suitcase roughly out of her way as she hurdled past the others and went upstairs. If they were waiting for her to get them upstairs, they were going to be waiting for awhile. She wasn't carrying anything without some help.

No one from the living room seemed to notice.

CHAPTER 4

Shanice hurried up the stairs to the end of the hall. Her bedroom was in the area above the garage— an addition added many years later to the old farmhouse. Shanice had been seven when her family moved in, and she had been fascinated by the little door at the end of the hallway that opened up into the gigantic unfinished space above the garage. The child-sized opening reminded her of the entrance to Wonderland after Alice fell down the rabbit hole.

When they moved in, wood planks had been placed sporadically over the insulated floor, and a single bare lightbulb hung haphazardly on a chain from the vaulted ceiling. The space smelled of cedar and fiberglass—the fragrance of old memories and new treasures for the little girl who loved to spend her summer afternoons in Grandma Leona's attic. Two tarnished circular windows overlooked the backyard. The room was frigid in the winter and so warm in the summer it took the breath out of you, but Shanice was drawn to the space. It was magical to her.

Two years later, her father decided the room over the garage would make a nice home office. After spending a few hundred dollars on a designer architectural plan to alter the little door, he discovered his daughter sobbing in her little hideaway in the back of the box-strewn storage area. The idea that he was going to replace her fairy-tale-sized door with a regular one was more than her nine year old could bear.

A year later, the space was officially Shanice's bedroom—with the three-foot door still intact.

She ducked as she entered and pushed the door closed behind her.

Mama had originally suggested that Tawny bunk with Shanice while she was there, but it was her dad who decided the two fifteen year olds would need their own separate spaces. They added a daybed to the home office where Tawny would stay. Jalin would room in the small guest bedroom next to Shanice's parents' room.

Her dad understood. He could sense the tension in the air between the two whenever they were together, even though Mama didn't seem to notice it, or didn't want to notice it. Shanice thought her dad might even understand why there was tension.

Crawling into bed, Shanice watched through her bedroom window as the trees swayed in the wind. The branches slipped into shadows as darkness rolled in. She grabbed her remote and flipped on the stereo. An older popular rock song about never being as big as Jesus burst forth.

This is a fun song. We should cover it.

She reached under her bed and found a spiral-bound notebook with a pen tucked inside. She jotted down a note about the song. She'd have to share it with the rest of the band the next day. Parker surely had it on CD somewhere—he had everything. And for what he didn't have, he had a way of knowing exactly who to go to in order to get it.

Turning the page, she found the words to the song she had been trying to perfect. Songwriting was new for her, but it was exhilarating to see her thoughts revealed on the page. Nibbling on the end of the pen, she read the words again:

> *Sometimes I feel kinda hopeless*
> *Sometimes I don't even know why I want to try*
> *Don't you know*
> *Sometimes I feel like giving it all up inside*
> *Sometimes I just want to cry out*
> *For the answers that I seek*
> *Sometimes I can't take any more of this*

(Can't keep it all inside)
I just need to be shown the way
And then it all comes together
When I see Your holy face.

With a sigh, she read them a second time. Tonight was the big night to spring them on Andria and see where they could take them from that point together. She had hinted about the lyrics to her friend, and Andria seemed enthusiastic about working on them together.

And then Andria's parents had decided to go to the family reunion at the last minute. . . .

The twins would be home soon, and then they could get to work.

She wanted to show her lyrics to Darby, but she didn't want to embarrass herself. That would be like handing over a stick-figure drawing to an art museum and expecting them to hang it beside a Monet or something. No, the lyrics had to be just right before the truly talented one of the bunch got to see them.

Tossing the notebook back under her bed, she rolled onto her back and flopped her head over the side. Parker's dazzling eyes caught her attention.

On the wall beside her bed hung a poster of Second Rate, the band Shanice sang backup vocals for. Her bright smiling face peeked out of the ball pit at McDonalds along with Parker, Elijah, Jenna Rose Brinley, and the twins, Andria and Darby McKennitt. Shanice and Jenna Rose were both hidden completely in the balls except for their faces. Parker was atop the slide that led into the pit while the others were goofing around in the balls.

That first photo shoot had been a great day. They had all wanted to bury themselves in the balls, but there wasn't enough room. Instead, they just played around until they were kicked out. For some reason, the manager didn't take to a group of teenagers hogging the little kids' playground, no matter what the reasoning.

The poster had been a recent gift from their manager/publicist,

Chance McKennitt. The twins' cousin was a college senior and had been a great boost to their entourage.

Entourage.

She found herself giggling at the thought of the word. Big stars had *entourages.* Garage bands had older cousins who drove vans. She'd have to share that thought with the rest of the band tomorrow as well. They'd all like the sound of it. Especially Chance.

Chance was more than just a cousin with a van. If it hadn't been for his motivation and vision, they would still be just a group of kids who liked to jam in the back of a pizza shop. Thanks to him, they had a successful gig under their belt, some real promotional stuff, and a date to record their first demo CD. Plus, they had three other gigs for the summer—one at a coffeehouse that could lead to a regular spot, the main act gig at a community picnic with two other bands, and a big-time youth rally opening for a major Christian band. Without Chance, none of that would have happened.

As she shook her foot nervously and stared dreamily at the picture of her and her friends, the realization that she hadn't sung all day and was feeling antsy because of it swept over her. The twins were doing the family thing and spending time at an aunt's house on the other side of the state until late this evening, and Amber, their soundboard operator, was at a church function. Jenna Rose had spent part of the day with Shanice and the two boys hanging out at the pizza shop, but when they decided to skate, she headed for home.

Today had been pretty much a waste.

As the time closed in on ten o'clock, Shanice made her way out of the room and down the hall to the restroom. She brushed her teeth and washed her face, then flipped off the light as she made her way into the office.

A green glow from the computer screen was the first thing that greeted her.

Oh man, Tawny.

Her cousin, looking annoyed, spun the computer chair around.

"You really need to knock," she stated.

"I need to use the computer," Shanice replied.

"I thought I was told this was my bedroom?"

Shanice sighed dramatically. "It is, but that's the only computer in the house. And I need to get on it. My friend should be home now, and we're supposed to chat."

"This is me caring. I'm using it." Tawny spun back around and continued clicking on items.

"What are you doing?"

"Downloading music," her cousin replied without turning around. An unedited hip-hop song blared loudly from the small speakers.

"You can't download stuff like that on my dad's computer."

"It's my room for the summer, so it's my computer for the summer. I left most of my CDs at home, and I need music somehow. I'm not listening to hymns or something all summer."

Shanice peered over her shoulder at the file full of song titles. File after file of gangsta rap and hard hip-hop. Her dad was going to flip and end up grounding both of them from the computer.

"I need the computer. I have a friend I need to talk to. Besides, my dad doesn't allow me to download that kind of music," she pleaded. "You're going to get us both in trouble."

"Why? Too black for your dad?" Tawny clicked on another raunchy file. "Or is it too black for you?"

Walk out of the room. Don't stoop to her level. Just get out.

Shanice couldn't bring herself to listen to the voice of reason in her head. She didn't know what Tawny's problem was, but she wasn't taking this all summer from her. Shanice leaned against the L-shaped desk and folded her arms like Mama always did when she meant business. She hoped Tawny caught the mimic in her actions. "What's your problem with me, Tawny? Because you've had a serious attitude since you got here."

Tawny spun the chair back around to face her. "You know, it's bad enough that I have to spend my summer in Whiteyville, but I came here and found the only black person my age wishing she was white. You tell me what's wrong."

Dumbfounded, Shanice struggled for the right words. She had to have some kind of response, but she couldn't come up with anything. Her heart raced and her mouth went dry.

Tawny rolled her eyes and turned back toward the computer screen. "I don't know what's more sorry," she mumbled. "The fact that you want to be white or the fact that you don't even see it."

Lord, help me out here.

Shanice twitched her foot as she tried to pull herself together. Part of her wanted to just scream at her cousin about how stupid she sounded, but the rest of her knew whatever answer she gave was probably going to have an impact on the rest of their summer. If they were going to have any chance of getting along over the next few months, they needed to work this out in a civilized manner.

But it didn't matter—the right words wouldn't come.

If Tawny couldn't see her for the person she was, Shanice would give her all the space she needed to be miserable all summer long. With a shake of her head, she quietly walked out the door.

Maybe her lack of drama would show Tawny how much she meant business this time.

Returning to her room, Shanice curled her legs up on her window seat and stared out into the night sky. The stars flickered between the windblown shadows of the clouds that passed by. The tall red maple in the McKennitt backyard swayed back and forth. Their homes were two of the oldest houses in town and still perched on two of the largest lots; their expansive backyards met at a gravel alley. She and Andria were too far apart to do walkie-talkies, can phones, or any of the other neat ways that two friends communicate in the really good books. It just wasn't quite fair.

Andria was now sitting at her computer and waiting to hear from her. They had to go over the lyrics that they had been working on, and Tawny, the spoiled brat, was in the office downloading music that would get Shanice into trouble.

Talking to Mama about it all probably wouldn't do much good. Shanice was pretty sure she would hear the you-need-to-work-it-out-yourself speech from her again. Mama had always been big on Shanice solving her own problems. She always told Shanice that standing on her own two feet and working things out instead of relying on others to intervene would make her a stronger woman. Most of the time, Shanice was glad Mama stayed out of things. It was a bit empowering to know that she could handle it all on her own.

Maybe she should have pushed for Tawny to sleep in her room while she was staying with them. The current setup wasn't really fair.

Tawny was in a room with the computer and a telephone, and Shanice wasn't allowed to have either one in her room. Not only was Shanice going to be cut off from reaching her friends, but Tawny was going to gloat that she could use it any time she wanted. If they were bunking together, at least she would be able to get online when she needed to.

Sitting here isn't going to solve anything.

Shanice hopped up and headed out of the room again. This time she went downstairs.

She wasn't sure what she was going to say, but she had to plead her case to someone. If nothing else, maybe she could get the computer moved to the kitchen, where it used to be, at least for the summer. That way she would have access to it as well.

Tawny was downstairs watching TV again.

Shanice turned and bolted back up the stairs. Grabbing the handle of the office door, she tried to turn it, but it wouldn't budge.

Locked? Huh?

"Dad!" she yelled.

She heard his footsteps on the foyer floor, heavy and long thumps, then listened as he made his way up the stairs two at a time. Quick, lighter footfalls followed. Tawny, no doubt.

"What's wrong?" he asked as he turned the corner on the landing and took the last three steps in one stride.

"The door's locked," she pleaded.

"I'm just used to having my door locked," Tawny explained as she mounted the last step.

Shanice's dad scratched his head and bent down to look at the doorknob. "I don't even have a clue where the key is to this thing. I don't think I've ever locked it before. It looks like just a little circle release."

"Oh, I know how to get it open," Tawny continued. "I lock the door at my house the same way. It's no big deal."

"I need to get in there," Shanice pleaded. "Andi is waiting on me, Dad. I need the computer."

"That's Tonya's room right now," her dad said carefully as he studied the lock. "I think she needs some time to get herself settled in before you need to be in there. We all need our own private space."

This is so unfair! I can't believe he's taking her side too.

"Well, what about me? Can I get my own computer then? I need to get on there."

"We've had that discussion before. Your mom and I don't see the need for you to have your own computer. It causes nothing but trouble when kids are left unchecked online."

Like I'm going to jump state with a thirty-five-year-old trucker or something. Give me some more credit than that, Dad. Besides, why does she get to go "unchecked" all summer?

"So Tawny gets a computer in her room, but I don't?" Stuffing her hands in her pockets, Shanice's shoulders slumped as she stared at her dad, waiting for an answer.

He said nothing in return.

"Can we at least get the computer out of there then?" she asked, feeling flabbergasted that even her dad was on her cousin's side instead of hers. "I need to use it."

"We'll have to take a look at it on the weekend and see what we can do."

"This weekend?"

That was still three days away.

He nodded, returning his attention to the locked door. "We'll have to figure out where to put it now that we redid the kitchen. That desk isn't going to come out of that room, and even if it did, there's no place else in the house to put it."

"We could put it on the kitchen table."

Desperate times, desperate measures. . .

"I think your mama would kill me for that one. We'll see what we can do."

Shanice leaned against the wall and stared in disbelief at her dad. Her own father had turned traitor on her.

He twisted the doorknob but it stayed fast. Tawny giggled as she returned downstairs.

"May I spend the night at Andi's then?" Shanice asked quietly.

He turned and looked at her. "I suppose, if it's okay with her folks." He watched her keenly for a moment. "You okay?" he probed.

If you have to ask, you obviously don't have a clue.

"Thanks. They never care," she replied. Without answering his question she plodded down the stairs.

CHAPTER 6

Shanice crossed the lawn in her socks, the dew dampening her toes with each step. It felt good on her weary feet. She still hadn't taken a shower, but she wasn't going back in her house to get one either. The McKennitts would let her use theirs. One sniff of her stinky body would do the trick. Girls may *glow* instead of sweat, they say, but skating definitely brought out the sweat on a hot June afternoon. The more she longed for a shower, the stickier she felt.

Maybe the McKennitts would let her stay with them all summer. They had the room. Their parents were both so busy with their work and traveling that they probably wouldn't even notice. Relief washed over her. Plus, Mrs. McKennitt loved having her around—they could talk about interior design and other stuff before the twins got up in the morning. They all had a lot in common. It was settled in her mind— she would ask if she could stay as often as possible as long as Tawny was here. Everyone would be happy that way.

She stopped and turned to look at her house again.

My house. My sanctuary.

Now Tawny and her perfect curls and Jalin and his adorable eyes had taken it over as their home.

Where did that leave her?

She crossed the forgotten gravel alleyway gingerly, mindful of her tender feet. Big clumps of grass shot out of the rocks. She tried to walk across them as best she could. No car had seen the alley in as long as she could remember. Her dad said that it was still there only as a fire passageway for trucks if needed. She couldn't recall ever seeing the alley used for that purpose either.

The twins' parents were seldom home together. Their mother, an interior designer, often worked on television sets and expensive homes, and their father was a businessman who traveled extensively. Shanice always wondered what could possibly be keeping two such successful adults in the little Ohio town where they were raised when it was obvious they could live just about anywhere they wanted. The brick executive home they owned had belonged to the twins' grandfather before them. They moved in when the twins were just seven—only two months after Shanice's family moved in.

Darby and Andria had become her best friends almost instantly. Their nanny, a burly German woman who spoke broken English, let them spend hours together in their adjoining backyards. It was the McKennitts who had led her family to the church they all called their own, the same place their music group Second Rate had gotten started. Regardless of their schedules, the Stevenson and McKennitt families were almost always at church together in the third pew on Sunday mornings.

Shanice smiled as she stuffed her hands back into her pockets and stepped into the McKennitt yard. It had been a long time since she had thought of the kind woman who had returned to Germany a few years back.

When she left, the twins were often left on their own after school. Their parents thought them responsible enough to care for themselves for a few hours. Mama would invite them over as much as possible, fretting over what they could be getting into unsupervised in such a large house. Personally, Shanice thought Mama watched too many movies from the 1980s about rich kids and their unsupervised partying. Her imagination was much wilder than anything Shanice and the girls could come up with to do in an afternoon.

For awhile, Mrs. McKennitt cut out nearly all her traveling so she could be home with the girls more. When she returned to work full time the same year the girls started high school, she explained to Shanice's mom that she wasn't "wired" to be the stay-at-home type like JaNay Stevenson was.

Mama did her best to watch over them, even now when both Shanice and the twins were fifteen. "Even good Christian kids are bound to get into trouble if given the time to find it," she would say. Shanice didn't believe either one of her friends knew how to even go looking for trouble. Darby and Andria would put on Goth-freak airs at times, but they were two of the sweetest, gentlest girls Shanice had ever known.

A strange shape in the back corner of the lot caught Shanice's eye as she neared the house. Between the shed and the willow tree, the trampoline that they had played on for years was now reassembled. Something was casting shadows across its top. Shanice squinted as she tried to make out the shapes.

A light came on in the kitchen, and she could hear heated voices from the open window drift into the night and fade away as the argument continued into another room. With the sound of those voices still fresh in her ears, Shanice made her way to the trampoline. As she drew closer, she could see her friends lying across the bouncy surface. Andria looked at her momentarily, her face full of emotion yet devoid of it at the same time, and then returned her gaze to the sky. Shanice hoisted herself up and found a spot between the twins.

Without a word, they all three turned their attention to the clouds flitting over the darkened sky and grasped hands, just as they had done hundreds of times since moving in beside one another. Shanice sighed heavily for her friends as the sounds of their parents' arguing returned and grew more intense. Andria squeezed Shanice's hand tighter until the voices faded away again.

I'm so sorry, guys. Sometimes there just aren't the right words. . . .

CHAPPTER 7

Shanice pulled a chair up alongside Darby, the taller twin, and set down a glass of soda in front of her. Darby was bent over a notebook and feverishly scrawling words across the page. Placing straws in both Darby's glass and her own, Shanice read the words over her friend's shoulder.

"Hey," Darby protested, throwing her arms across the page.

Shanice lightly bopped her friend on the head and took the seat next to her. "Don't go writing it in front of me if you don't want me to read it, you dork."

From the back of the building, the phone rang as the sounds of the pizza shop sounded around them. Andria jumped up to answer the phone for the Angelinos. The chain that hung from her pants rattled like Christmas bells as she hurried over.

The pizza shop was a favorite gathering spot for many of the teens in town, but it held a special place in the hearts of the band members. They gathered every day to practice and play music for anyone who wandered into the back room that was saved especially for their use. And as the relatives and guardians of their bandmate Elijah, the Angelinos were like family.

Darby kept a protective arm over her notebook and swatted playfully at Shanice. "No peeking," she whined. "You can't see it yet."

"We all know it's awesome, Darb," Shanice said, knowing full well that she might never see the words to Darby's latest poem. Darby kept most of her work to herself, and what the rest of the group did get to see was usually smuggled out by her sister.

Darby's long brown hair hung like a protective wall around the paper as she shook her head a second time. Folding the cover of the notebook closed, she stuffed it into her backpack.

"We need to get that one down to some music," Andria said as she returned from taking the pizza order. "I've seen it. It's good."

Darby snickered, embarrassed, and took a long drag of her soda. "Do you ever notice that we're always sitting around waiting for the guys?" she asked, trying to change the subject.

Her sister wasn't buying it. "Yeah, we do, and we still need to put that one down to music. We need some more of our own music if we're ever going to go anywhere. Covering worship songs and all is cool enough, but if we're ever going to get there on our own, we need to get a sound all our own."

Wrapping her arms around her friend's shoulders, Shanice hugged Darby tightly. "And that means you," she added. She held on just a moment longer, hoping that her friend realized her gesture meant so much more than simple encouragement about her songwriting abilities.

Andria was not a hugger. The handgrip they had shared the night before was the closest sign of affection she would give—especially in a stressful situation. She seldom showed her affectionate side even to Elijah, her boyfriend, Shanice had noticed. Darby, on the other hand, craved that kind of physical attention. Shanice tried to reach out to her two friends respective of their individual needs as much as she could. She knew that need was somewhat neglected with their parents being gone so much of the time.

A blond with her hair pulled back into a ponytail walked through the door and waved at the trio around the table. She wore a pair of aged black jeans and a white baby doll shirt with an old cartoon character printed on it.

Darby returned the wave.

Shanice smiled as she watched the newcomer. Just a few months ago when Jenna Rose Brinley had come into their lives, Shanice was sure she was some snobby prep who had little interest in them except for their guitarist, Parker. For the most part, she had been right, but not anymore. Jenna Rose had changed for the better, and now she was one of Shanice's best friends. Of course, she still had her preppy moments, but all in all, she was one of them.

Jenna Rose thanked sweet, round Mrs. Angelino with a big hug as the kind woman handed her a diet soda. She then joined the other girls at the table.

"Have fun skating last night?" Jenna Rose asked Shanice as she took the chair across from her.

Shanice nodded and tugged at her red do-rag. Dressed in a white tank top, her favorite pair of camos cut off just below the knee, and orange flip-flops, she prided herself on always looking just a little different from everyone else.

"I always do," she replied, "and I *will* get you out there."

Jenna Rose chuckled. "Only if they have training wheels on them. I don't get how anyone can stand on those things."

"Hey, even Barbie skates," Shanice teased.

Jenna Rose stuck out her tongue in return.

Music poured unexpectedly from the back room where their instruments were set up.

Andria smiled and shook her head in disbelief. "Did anyone even know Amber was here?"

"That girl is a freak," Shanice replied, meaning the word to be a compliment. Amber Smith was the real genius behind the band, or so Parker always said. Shanice didn't believe anyone would disagree with him. A second-generation musician, Amber had a gift for knowing how to arrange the music to get the best sound. No one ever dared argue music with the quiet girl who was such a special part of Second Rate.

"Let's go on in then," Darby added, showing great eagerness to get to her guitar. "Who needs boys anyway?"

"I know I do," her sister stated simply.

Darby smacked her on the arm and giggled. "Oh, Elijah," she sang dreamily.

The four girls all laughed as they followed Darby through the door. Jenna Rose flipped Shanice's braids and wrapped an arm around her shoulder. Shanice returned the gesture as they entered the back room.

Andria pulled off her Christian band tee to reveal a fitted tank underneath. She tossed her shirt on a chair and headed toward her drums. Kicking off her shoes, she took her seat and twirled her drumsticks in the air. One stick clattered to the ground before she smiled sheepishly and picked it up.

"You need to work on that," Jenna Rose kidded her.

Andria smirked and twirled the drumstick again.

Shanice positioned her microphone as Amber bobbed her head from behind the soundboard, her heavy earphones covering her ears. "Amber!" she called out. "Share the wealth, dawg. Whatcha listening to?"

Amber pulled down the earphones and flipped off a switch. "I'm just playing around with 'Awesome God' and some techno beats—nothing serious."

Everyone broke into laughter.

"That's one song I never pictured techno," Darby admitted as she plucked at the strings of her guitar to get the correct pitch.

"Oh, I like techno," Parker said as he stepped into the room. "What about techno?"

Swaggering in wearing blue work pants and a white tee that clung to his chest, Parker set his guitar case on a table. Elijah, dressed nearly the same way, followed.

"Hey," Darby called, thumbing back and forth between herself and her sister, "I thought we were the twins?"

Elijah flicked her ear playfully as he passed by. Wrinkling his nose at his girlfriend Andria, he grabbed up his bass guitar and turned on his amp. He was noticeably thinner than Parker. Short, dark stubble covered Elijah's head—the remnants of a dye job gone bad, and his black square-framed glasses completed his look. Parker had the cover-boy look going, but Elijah was about pure rock and roll. Shanice liked that about him.

"I always knew I was a trendsetter," Elijah said with a smile, "but the boy's got issues! He's like peeking in my windows or something to see what I'm wearing. It's a bit creepy, dude."

Parker just shook his head and laughed as everyone settled down. Before every practice, they prayed as a group, and he generally started it. "Lord," he said, closing his eyes, "this is all for You, Lord. When it stops being about You and for You, Lord, take it all away."

"Help us live by faith and not by our sight, Lord," Darby added.

"These gifts are from You and for You, Lord," Elijah continued. "May they be pleasing to You and work for Your kingdom."

Andria cleared her throat, emotion choking her words. "I lay it all at Your feet, Jesus," she whispered. "All that I have and all that I am, I give to You."

Shanice's heart ached for her friend. Silently, she added a prayer for Him to watch over them and heal the pains that had plagued their house and tested them for so long. For as long as she had known the twins, the fighting had gone on between their parents. Shanice couldn't imagine living in that atmosphere for so long, especially when you were expected to put on a charade for the rest of the world. They had all gotten so good at the pretending that they were starting to believe it was real.

But God had to require more of a marriage than just not divorcing.

"Lord, You are beautiful," Shanice whispered aloud, fighting the urge to go hug her friend that very moment. "You have given me so much, Lord, and I praise You for it. Please, Lord, give me the perseverance to deal with the things that are out of my control and the patience to show Your love in my actions."

"Jesus, I pray I need You every day and forever," Amber finished before they all said "amen" together.

Jenna Rose simply added an amen. She had yet to join in the prayer time, but no one was forcing her. She'd do it in her own time, Shanice knew. It seemed pretty evident that she was a newer Christian and perhaps not ready to pray publicly. Shanice couldn't imagine what it would be like to be a preacher's child; everyone probably just assumed Jenna Rose had a relationship with Christ. It had to be a difficult place to be in.

As Andria started them up with the drum track, Shanice gripped her microphone tightly and bobbed her head to the beat. Her thoughts went back to her own situation at home. She had to make a better effort to get along with Tawny. . .even though things were a bit rougher than the last time they saw each other. They hadn't gotten off to the best start this time, but she wasn't the one whose life was being torn apart by fighting parents. She couldn't imagine what Tawny and Jalin were going through.

I thought it. I prayed it. Now I just gotta do it.

That little mocking voice in the back of her mind didn't want to let her forget that Tawny wasn't going to make it easy for her.

Digging through the garage, Shanice searched for the basketball that had been long forgotten. She really hated basketball. Tawny, on the other hand, loved it and played at her school in Detroit. Like starter-on-a-championship-team kind of played. Hoops were important to her, and even though Shanice despised the game, she couldn't dismiss the fact that they had enjoyed a lot of fun over the years while playing together. On her way home from band practice, the idea came to her that basketball might be the way the two cousins could reconnect. At least she would give it a try.

There was no way she was going the whole summer without trying to get somewhere with Tawny. Contrary to what her friends might have thought, Shanice hated conflict. She especially hated *dragged-out* conflict. Get it out in the open, get it worked out, and get on with it—that was the way she liked to deal with things.

Her heart was screaming at her to stick with the routine—open her journal, reflect, and sing. After every practice, she would return to the solitude of her room and spend some time with her thoughts as she pondered the events of the day. Most days it would just lead to her working on her voice and learning the songs, but lately her thoughts were coming out in lyrical form.

She was finally starting to understand Darby's attitude toward her notebook a bit. Those lyrics in her notebook were part of Shanice's soul, and she guarded them intensely. Andria was the only one who even knew that Shanice was trying her hand at songwriting.

It had been so important to her to instant message on the computer last night. With every night of practice, her lyrics were maturing and developing into the kind of material that Darby created. Shanice started writing thinking she could bring Darby out of her shell a bit—get her to share her songs so they could record more of them. Instead, she found herself becoming more private about her own feelings.

The basketball rolled out from behind a forgotten wheelbarrow as she pushed it aside.

Scooping up the ball, Shanice hurried into the house to find her cousin.

"Up for some hoops?" she asked as she entered the living room.

Sprawled out on the living room floor, Jalin was asleep. Cartoon music blared from the television in front of him, much louder than Mama ever let her watch television. He stirred lightly at the sound of her voice.

Tawny was again draped over the sofa, this time with the phone plastered to one ear. She sat up quickly and gave Shanice a dirty look.

Who is she talking to? Don't tell me she's allowed to make long-distance calls too. Man, this is all so unfair.

"Can't you see that the baby's asleep?" Tawny shot back as she returned to her relaxed position.

"Sorry, Jalin," Shanice whispered as she shifted the ball from one arm to the other. He didn't flinch. Satisfied that he was sleeping soundly again, she returned her attention to Tawny. "So, you game or what?"

"Where we playing?"

Shanice almost choked as she kept herself from laughing. If Tawny thought they were going to find some ballers at the park courts, she was in for the shock of her life. There was a reason their high school boys' team was 2–12 last year, and it had a lot to do with the fact that most guys at her school thought *dribbling* was something you did with a soccer ball. If they were going to scope the park, they might be lucky to find a couple of thug-wannabe seventh graders there in saggy shorts and imitation throwback jerseys. Probably they would front for the attention of a *real-life* urban chick.

That might be fun to watch. . .but it'd be too cruel.

"Just here, I guess," Shanice replied. "We got the hoop in the drive. There's really no place worth going to this late just to play one-on-one."

Tawny rolled her eyes and shook her head in response. "Yeah, I thought something like that would be your excuse." Turning her attention back to the person on the other side of the phone, she said, "You see what I'm going through down here?"

Lord, let me hit her just once!

No, no, just calm yourself down.

Tawny's presence was putting her alter ego into overdrive.

"Excuse for what?" Shanice shifted her weight from one leg to the other and gripped the ball until her knuckles turned white. "You want to sit in here on the couch all summer? Go for it. Don't think I'm spending it sitting beside you."

Tawny smacked her lips and turned her eyes toward the wall.

"You are so not worth it," sighed Shanice as she fled from the room.

Before this summer's over, I'm going to kill her. Forgive me for it now, but I am.

Tawny's shrill laughter was the last sound she heard as she slammed the back door and headed toward the McKennitt house.

M usic streamed from the trampoline as Shanice stepped into the yard. Jenna Rose, her bare feet flopped over the edge, waved her over. A pair of sunglasses pulled her hair back from her face. Dressed in a pair of faded jean shorts and a sleeveless light blue top, she looked as if she were posing for one of the teen magazine covers. It was probably only a matter of time before she adorned one. Jenna Rose reached over the side of the trampoline to the stereo propped in a lawn chair and changed CDs as Shanice crossed the lawn.

Darby scooted over so their friend could hop up on the rubber mat. "We were wondering how long it was going to take you to get over here," she said as she fell backward. Her hair spread wildly around her. Darby was clad in the yellow Transformer shirt the girls had vowed to share from their first shopping trip as a band. Shanice was a bit jealous—Darby looked as good in it as Jenna Rose did. Shanice didn't plan on wearing it again, not after seeing how the shirt fit those two.

With a shrug, she bumped her shoulder playfully against Andria's arm. Her friend smiled as she continued to stare off into the grass. "What's up, woman?" Shanice asked.

This time Andria shrugged. "Life, I guess." She twisted her finger around the chain that hung from her knee-length green cutoffs. As was customary for their drummer, she wore a white tank top. Today her red-dyed hair lay flat except for her bangs, which were spiked out at an angle from her forehead.

"Our dad needs to hurry off on his next business trip," Darby explained. "He's golfing today, but mom's in such a mood from him even being here all week that we don't want to be in there."

Shanice nodded, again fighting off the urge to wrap her arms around her friends. Yet she didn't want to make Darby and Andria feel more uncomfortable, so she kept her thoughts to herself. "So we're hanging out here tonight?"

"Pizza's on the way," Andria replied as a wide smile crossed her face.

"Of course that's going to bring a smile to her face," Jenna Rose retorted, sharing a look with Shanice. Having pizza delivered to the trampoline meant Elijah was working delivery. Nobody else in town got such preferential treatment.

Of course, probably no one else in town got free pizza.

Andria tried to dart a dirty look at Jenna Rose, but instead it came out as a silly grin.

"We all know the truth."

Andria sighed and fell backward on the trampoline. Cans of pop rolled across the surface as her momentum tipped over the box.

No one in the circle of friends really knew how long Elijah and Andria had been a couple. To Shanice, it seemed like their whole life. Thinking of a time without them together just seemed wrong. They weren't one of those gross PDA couples who hung all over each other all day long, nor were they the average I-can't-spend-an-hour-without-him teenage romance. There was so much more between them—they were soul mates.

"And we got the Dew," Darby added, tossing a green can her way. Shanice caught it and stuffed it between her knees.

"We're set," she laughed.

"Except we need some chocolate," Jenna Rose said. "Think 'Lijah will hook us up?"

Andria nodded as she opened a can herself. " 'Lijah's always got the hookup," she said slyly, then burst into laughter. Laughing with her, Jenna Rose passed along her cell phone, and Andria dialed the number to the pizza shop.

"Who's that in your window?" Darby asked, squinting toward the Stevenson home.

Everyone's attention turned from Andria's phone call to Shanice's house. Tawny ducked out of the upstairs window as Shanice scrambled across the trampoline's surface to get a better view.

"Was it a little kid?" she asked.

"No. It was a girl."

"She wasn't in my room, was she?"

Darby looked up at the house again. "No. That's the bathroom, isn't it?" She pointed to a smaller window. The curtains still swayed.

Tossing the phone back to Jenna Rose, Andria strained to look up at the window. "He's bringing us chocolate. Who is she, 'Nice, and why are you keeping her locked up in the house?"

Relieved, Shanice lay back down on the mat. "That would be my cousin. And yeah, that's the bathroom."

"That boy rocks!" Turning to Shanice, Jenna Rose changed the subject back. "Why doesn't she come out and join us?" She ran her fingers through her long blond hair as the wind tossed it across the front of her face.

See that shampoo-ad hair-flippy thing you do? That's why.

"We're too white for her," Shanice mumbled in return.

Andria broke into a fit of laughter. "Too white? Sister, have you looked in the mirror lately?"

"Obviously I don't see what she does," Shanice replied as she mockingly surveyed her dark arms. "I don't know. She's had a bad attitude the last couple times I've seen her, and I don't think it's getting any better. She's going to be here all summer, I guess."

"Is she going to hang out in your bathroom all summer looking at us?" Jenna Rose asked.

If we're lucky. If she stays up in the bathroom, that means she won't be down here trashing us all day.

"I think we should invite her over," Darby stated. "There's always room for one more on the trampoline."

Amber appeared on her bicycle, pedaling haphazardly through the rocky alley.

Oh well. Amber makes one more. No room now. . .

"Hey, guys," Amber called as her front tire wobbled its way through the stones.

She's going to kill herself.

While Amber was a musical genius, coordination was not one of her other strong attributes. The others watched her approach with baited anticipation for a disaster, but she made it without incident.

"Did you bring chocolate?" Jenna Rose asked as she made room for her friend.

"What is up with you and chocolate?" Shanice asked. "How can you stay so skinny with chocolate on the brain all day long?"

Jenna Rose pulled her legs up to her chest and wrapped her arms around them. "Blessed, I guess. Most of the time it's just on my brain and not in my mouth."

"I love this song," Amber said as she parked her bike.

"Of course you do," Andria replied impatiently. "Name me a song you don't like. Did you bring chocolate?"

"If it twangs, I don't like it. No chocolate. It's like a hundred degrees outside, and I rode my bike. Any chocolate on me would be just that—melted *on* me." She tried to pull herself up on the platform, but she couldn't quite get there. Andria and Jenna Rose both grabbed an arm and pulled her up.

"Amen to that, sister. Down with the twang," Shanice nodded, retrieving a can from the box and rolling it toward the newcomer. "Dude, is 'Lijah bringing more pop too?"

"Be thankful he's bringing us pizza," Andria replied.

As Amber opened her soda, fizz poured over the edge and onto her shirt. She put it to her lips and sucked at the bubbles, but the front of her red tank top was soaked all the same.

"Man, you're like a mess magnet, aren't you?" Shanice laughed lightly at her friend. She just loved Amber. The chubby girl who always kept her mouse-brown hair in a ponytail was one of the most thoughtful and unselfish people Shanice had ever met. Amber had been the first person to befriend Shanice when her family moved here.

And you looked different from everyone else, but she didn't even care about that. Just like Tawny must feel right now.

Shanice looked again toward the window. Maybe she should invite her cousin out. She was probably in there surfing on *her* computer or talking long-distance on *her* phone. Or doing something else the Stevensons wouldn't allow their own daughter to do.

She probably won't come anyway.

Maybe she wouldn't. Either way, Shanice knew she should at least invite Tawny. The memory of being new and looking different flooded back—bringing feelings and thoughts she hadn't relived in a long time. She had been seven when they moved to this new town with different-colored skin and parents who looked nothing like each other. She could only imagine what it must be like at fifteen, being fully aware of the ways people *might* treat you based on the color of your skin.

"So," Jenna Rose broke the silence, "where's she from?"

"Who?" Shanice shook her head, waking up from her daze. "Oh, Tawny. Detroit."

"Tawny?" Darby asked. "Tawny's here? I remember her. I didn't know it was Tawny visiting. She's pretty cool."

Taking a long drag of her drink, Shanice shook her head. "She's not like she used to be, Darb. She's like a stereotype thug chick now. . .attitude and all. Thirty seconds with her is five minutes too long."

"I remember that one summer she was here for a couple of weeks," Andria reminisced. "She was a riot. We had a blast."

"Well, I'm moving in with you guys for the summer because she's driving me nuts."

Andria's gaze returned longingly to her house. All was quiet inside at the moment. "Yeah, well, you might just want to take your chances with Tawny," she replied softly.

CHAPTER 110

You know," Andria said as she put her slice of pizza on her lap and watched the light come on in her kitchen window, "I wish my parents would see that they're living an image instead of a life. That can't be what God intended for their marriage to be like."

Nah, Andi, look at my mom and dad. That's how it's supposed to be. They have love and compromise, friendship and compassion. It's one big happy Brady Bunch *episode every day.* But Shanice couldn't bring herself to voice the thought. It seemed too much like bragging or something.

"Why do they stay together then?" Amber asked as she searched for a napkin. Finally, she just wiped her hands on the sides of her jean shorts.

"It would look too bad if they weren't, I suppose," Andria replied. "It's all about the image with them."

"I think they want to make it work," Darby said in a voice filled with hope, "but they don't know how. Or they've long forgotten why to keep trying."

"I just know I'm not going to live my life like that," Andria concluded.

Another light came on upstairs. Their mother's figure passed before the window.

"Just look at them," Andria continued. "They're on opposite sides of the house all the time. If they're ever home together at the same time, they're nowhere near each other."

"And if they are, they're fighting," Darby added.

Andria nodded. "I just know Elijah and I aren't going to live like that. I don't care if we're millionaires. We aren't going to live in a house where we can hide from each other and our problems. We're going to have a cozy little house where we are forced to deal with each other and any arguments that come up."

Amber reached around and rubbed Andria's back as she spoke. "We'll just keep praying that they see it like you guys do."

A pink streak burst across the sky as the sun dipped in the horizon. Shanice held her breath and marveled at its beauty. The others grew quiet as well. The chirp of the crickets in the bushes and a neighbor's lawn mower filled the night air as the CD clicked off. The girls all stared off into the coming night sky.

The silence was a bit unnerving. Shanice wanted to grab a CD. More music. Music meant fun. Music meant they were the best of friends having the best of times.

What song would be fitting for this moment in the soundtrack of our lives?

But at the same time, the silence was good. The silence brought out so much more to their friendship. Friends like these were based on more than just the good times. Real friendships were built on the cornerstones of these quiet, contemplative moments together—moments when they listened to God—and Shanice felt good about having friends with the same beliefs and with whom she could share that special bond. Most kids didn't seem to be so fortunate. They were too concerned with trivial things, and their friendships seldom lasted past the first storm.

Her thoughts returned again to her cousin sitting alone in the house. How many of these kind of nights had she had? It was no surprise to anyone in the family when Tawny's parents announced they were divorcing. The relationship had been extremely ugly for as long as Shanice could remember. Family reunions and other gatherings were no different. Those two didn't care about the image at all. They fought and belittled each other every chance they could get. They almost seemed to live for upsetting one another.

Quietly, Shanice observed Andria fiddling again with the chain on her pants and staring into the sky. How many times had Tawny sought refuge from her parents' arguments by staring off into the sky? And where did she go to get away from their heated voices? She lived in a townhouse in the middle of the city. She had no yard and the city lights had to force out the night sky. So where did she go? Where was her getaway?

She came to my house.

"Maybe I should go see if she wants to come out and join us," Shanice whispered aloud to no one in particular.

Amber hopped off the trampoline. "I'll go with you," she said kindly.

Good old Amber. She wasn't even here to know what I'm talking about, yet she's willing to back me up.

Shanice kicked off her flip-flops, anticipating the cool dew on her toes, but the night was too warm. The grass, watered each morning by an underground system, was soft and lush. She kept her shoes off anyway. Mama always said she inherited wanting to be barefoot from her southern roots. Those roots must run deep, because Mama's grandparents were from Detroit as well. Mama was about as far removed from the South as one could get.

As long as the grass wasn't dry and scratchy, Shanice preferred to go without her shoes.

They crossed the yards without a word. Amber was one of those people who preferred to listen rather than talk. Shanice had tried often to get her to open up a bit instead of always just dumping on her, but Amber was steadfast in her position. It was like the girl enjoyed her role as a sponge—take everything in and only let it back out at the right time. Being silent with Amber was normal and much less daunting.

Mama greeted them in the kitchen as she loaded the dishwasher. "Not in search of leftovers, I presume," she said as she closed the door and the machine hummed to life.

"We had a pizza," Shanice replied, snagging a cold bottle of water from the fridge. She offered one to Amber, who politely refused.

"It's a wonder you girls don't weigh twice what you do with all the pizza you eat. The Angelinos are good people, but they'd be millionaires if they'd start charging you kids for all the stuff you eat there. Good people and good business sense seldom go together."

Mama folded her towel neatly, placed it on the counter, and turned to face the girls. "So how are you, Amber?"

"Fine, Mrs. Stevenson," she replied dutifully. "Thank you."

"Sweetie, are you ever going to do anything with that hair of yours?" Mama came forward and ran her fingers through Amber's ponytail as the girl smiled and tossed her head awkwardly. This scene was played out every time Amber came home with Shanice.

Mom! You are so embarrassing!

Shanice tried to catch Mama's attention. Did she even know how embarrassing she was?

Mama continued, "You girls are hardly little girls anymore. The best way to start feeling like a young lady is to start looking the part." She flashed a look at her daughter. "All of you need to start thinking of that. . .especially with your musical aspirations. I'd like to see you look as good as you sing."

Yeah, whatever, Mama.

Amber bounced her bangs nervously and shuffled her feet. "If I could ever decide what to do with it, I would cut it."

Again, Mama touched her hair. "This has some serious body in it, doesn't it? Shanice's hair is very full like that." She glanced at her daughter again, her tone becoming sharper. "If she'd do something with it, it'd be gorgeous."

Here it comes. The whole if-I'd-just-act-like-a-girl-I'd-be-prom-queen speech. . .

"You know what you need, honey? A black hairdresser. A black hairdresser will get this body under control for you. No one knows frizz and curls like we do." She stepped back, looking over the ponytail she had teased and poofed into gigantic proportions. "I tell you what, Tawny and I are going to the salon tomorrow afternoon. You should join us." Her eyes fell on her daughter as well. "You *both* should come."

Tawny is going to the salon? Tawny and my mama are going out to do things and I'm being invited along as an afterthought?

Shanice was floored. Her mouth hung open as she looked at her mama in disbelief. Mama was still fussing over Amber's mane of hair.

I had no real problem with them coming to stay with us, but now they're "going places" too?

She could see Tawny in the living room, her perfect head of perfect curls with the gold highlights glowing under the light of the lamp behind her. Filing at a fingernail, she was curled up in the big comfy chair Shanice's dad favored. Even in her pajamas, Tawny looked like a cover girl.

Shanice's heart raced as the thought of Tawny and Mama spending those "girl" moments together whisked through her head. She could picture them sitting in front of a mirror, talking about *black people* hair and *black people* makeup techniques and all those other things she didn't share in common with Mama.

Mama wanted a black queen for a daughter, and instead she got a tan tomboy with frizzy white-textured hair and a freckly face.

Yeah, well, looks like Mama finally got her prom queen.

The humidity hung thick in the air as Shanice rolled out of bed the next morning. Patches of sunbeams lay motionless on her bedroom floor.

Today has to be a swimming day.

Second Rate was getting together in the evening to go over their set and pick up the flyers Chance was making for their coffeehouse gig up north on Saturday. Until then, she was swimming. Her friends could join her if they wanted—she didn't care. Her old house wasn't air-conditioned like all of theirs, so she had no refuge from the heat. And with the likelihood of Tawny hogging the sofa and the remote all day, she wasn't hanging out here any longer than she had to.

Still in her pajamas, she prepared her bag for the pool: a black tankini with white stripes on the bottoms, sunscreen, two beach towels, and a pair of red soccer shorts.

Someone knocked lightly.

Mama opened the door without waiting for a response and ducked through the small opening. "Good morning," she said cheerily.

"Good morning," Shanice replied. She found it surprising Tawny wasn't on her Mama's heels already.

"So what's on your agenda for the day?" She sat down in the maple rocking chair with the cane-weaved seat that Shanice had salvaged from Grandma Leona's attic. Shanice's room was full of treasures from her grandma's house. "Are you coming to the salon with us?"

"I wanted to go swimming," she replied as she dug through her armoire for her "Christian girl" tank top.

"It would be nice if you went to the salon. It might give you a chance to connect with your cousin again."

"My braids are fine. I'll get them done again in a few days."

Please let that be a good enough reason. . . .

Pulling a red bandanna over her head, she secured her braids away from her face.

"That's not really what I meant, Shanice. The two of you need some common ground again—we need to do something you both enjoy to get you two reacquainted. It'll do you both good. You were close for so long. I hate to see you ruin that."

"And just how is the beauty salon going to do that, Mama? I don't care about getting my hair done. Or my nails. Or makeup either. None of that stuff is important to me. So why am I the one who has to do what she likes?"

Mama got to her feet and opened the door. "Because she's your guest. We're going to the salon at three. I expect to see you home and ready to go."

She's not my guest. Who said I wanted her here?

Mama closed the door gently behind her.

Shanice dropped her bag to the floor and flung herself back on her bed. Playing basketball was doable. Pretending she was interested in hip-hop videos was doable. Listening to a bunch of cackling loud women "Amen, sister" one other as they gossiped was not the way she was willing to try to connect.

She came in asking me if I wanted to go and left telling me that I was. Not fair.

At least Amber could save her. Hopefully she was going too. She could convince her to go. Amber's presence would take the edge off and hopefully force Tawny to behave herself.

She scooped her stuff back up and headed toward the door. The pool opened in a couple of hours, so she'd get some skating in before swimming. If she showed up at the salon smelling of sweat and chlorine, maybe they'd ask her to leave. Those prissy old gossips at the salon wouldn't stand for a stinkpot in their place.

Tawny exited the bathroom as Shanice pulled her door shut. "Don't you feel stupid with that little kiddie door still?" she asked. For the first time, her voice wasn't harsh or condescending. She was simply curious.

"No way," Shanice replied. "That's my room—I love it just the way it is." She wanted to remind her cousin that there was a time when she thought it was the coolest place in the world too. The first time Tawny had spent a week with her family, the two girls had sneaked out of bed together and sat up late into the night in the unfinished room telling ghost stories by flashlight. Hidden in the floor under her bed was the metal time capsule they had put together as the room was being finished. A picture of the two of them with their arms around each other was the highlight of the tin box. The room wasn't just part of Shanice's history—it was part of Tawny's too.

Reminding her would probably cause a fight.

"Have you painted or anything lately?" Tawny asked, catching Shanice by surprise.

Okay, what are you up to?

Shanice studied her for a moment, unsure of her sudden interest in her room. "No," she replied. "It's still the same."

"Not much around here has changed," Tawny replied as she surveyed the hall full of pictures of Shanice's elementary school past. Pictures of both of them as little girls playing together were scattered among them. "Your ma likes things the way she likes them, huh?"

Shanice almost laughed. That was an understatement. Mama had her ways and she wasn't much for trying new ones. Their house had hardly changed except for the kitchen remodel five years ago. Mama set everything up the way she wanted it, and that's the way it needed to be. *Order* was Mama's favorite word.

There was a bit of sorrow again in Tawny's face as she opened the door to the office and disappeared inside. Every time they had gone to

Michigan to visit Grandma Leona and Mama's other relatives, Shanice had noticed that her aunt Tiesha lived in a different place. Everything about each house or apartment was different too—different furniture, different decor, everything. And sometimes Uncle Antony lived with them and other times he did not. Tawny would have a totally different room each time—new bed, new decorations—and Shanice would be so jealous. Tawny would have all kinds of cool new stuff, while Shanice had the same old boring stuff she had always had.

You should ask her to go swimming with you.

She pushed the idea away as quickly as it came to her. Tawny hated being in the sun. She would just whine the whole time about getting "too dark" if she did go. When the extended family got together, Tawny and an older cousin would huddle under a tree to hide from the sun's rays and whine about "getting too black," while the other cousins, including Shanice, played games outside. It seemed awfully strange coming from someone who was always pestering her to accept that *she* was black.

Therein lay the problem. When Shanice looked in the mirror, she didn't see more black than white. Shanice didn't see one or the other, but she didn't really see herself as biracial either. She was Shanice—nothing more, nothing less. Her great-great-grandfather's written history began when he purchased his wife's freedom, they escaped to Michigan, and he changed his name to Douglas Tubman in honor of the two black anti-slavery activists. On her father's side, her great-grandfather, Jan Sutphen, had escaped Nazi occupation and taken the name of the man who had processed his papers upon entering America. "Stevenson" seemed much more American than "Sutphen" to him—especially in a time when it was not favorable to be German.

Trying to run from your real identity seemed to be a common thread through both sides of her family history. But Shanice had decided some time ago that the running would stop with her. She wasn't going to deny who she was. Neither history was less significant than the other; neither history was more important than the other.

Except when she was around her black cousins, Shanice saw her skin as nothing more than that—skin. Its color defined her no more than the color of her house defined that building's character. Every time her cousins were around, it became painfully evident that race mattered to some people much more than it should.

Shaking herself out of her daze, she bounded down the steps and into the kitchen.

Mama was hovering over the counter, her tiny nephew standing on a chair at her side. His shorts hung loosely around his hips, exposing the top of his diaper, and his chest was bare. He was popping pieces of strawberry into his mouth faster than Mama could clean them.

Mama didn't even turn around as Shanice entered the room. "Good morning," she said, as if the conversation in the bedroom earlier had been Shanice's imagination. Maybe it had.

Shanice crossed the room and stole a strawberry out of the colander. "When'd you go get these?" she asked, tossing it into her mouth. Its sweet juices brought an explosion of hunger to her stomach.

"Jalin and I went to the berry patch yesterday," she replied, tousling her nephew's hair. He continued to eat without a word.

We always went to the berry patch together. Me and my mama.

One of Shanice's fondest memories of her childhood was of her and Mama donning the big straw hats Mama had hung on the side porch and heading just outside of town to the strawberry fields. The old farmer who owned them, clad in baggy bib overalls and a wide straw hat of his own, would direct them to the rows where they were allowed to pick. Shanice would always choose the line of plants on the end and longingly eye the berries visible in the rows they weren't supposed to pick. Those berries always looked bigger and sweeter, no matter what the size of the ones she was tossing in her basket. Her mind would wonder how they must taste, but she was never brave enough to snitch one. The man in the overalls was sure to be angry. She couldn't imagine what such a tall man would do when he was angry.

Now this little cousin was eating the strawberries after Mama washed them. That was her thing to do. She was the one who was supposed to watch over Mama's hands and steal the ones that looked like they must be the sweetest. Her resentment grew steadily.

Quiet little twerp hardly ever speaks, but he's trouble.

A sinking feeling in the pit of her stomach told her that these cousins of hers were cutting into more than her summer. . . .

CHAPTER 12

Three o'clock," Mama called as Shanice headed out the door.

Yeah, yeah.

She slid her feet into her skates and headed down the driveway.

Mama opened the back door and called for her. Shanice almost continued on, pretending like she didn't hear her, but she knew she would catch it later if she tried something like that. Mama didn't take well to disobedience. And she would get even more upset about Shanice ignoring her.

She turned and headed back toward the house.

"Where are you off to?" Mama asked, wiping her hands on her pink-stained apron.

"The pool," she replied, knowing that she couldn't make up another story with her beach towel hanging out of the back of her bag. She wanted to tell her something else—some place where she was sure her cousin wouldn't want to go.

"I'll make a deal with you. If you take Jalin to the pool, you don't have to come to the salon yet."

Babysitting? You've got to be kidding!

It didn't sound like much of a deal to her. Spending the day in the wading pool with a two year old just couldn't compare even to the beauty salon. At least in the salon she'd have air-conditioning instead of boiling in warm two-feet-deep water.

"He'd have much more fun with you," Mama continued. "I don't think he'd enjoy the salon."

You know I don't enjoy the salon, yet you're still willing to make me go!

"I wanted to skate for awhile first," she wheedled, trying to weasel her way out.

"Well, skate for awhile then come back and get him. You can take the stroller."

"I don't want anyone to see me pushing a stroller," Shanice whined.

"What? Afraid someone might think he's yours? They'd have to think you were a girl first." Mama chuckled to herself, obviously thinking that her comment was a joke, but Shanice didn't find the humor in it.

"Whatever, Mama," she whispered. "I'll be back in a bit."

Mama returned inside, still chuckling at herself.

Shanice skated away, stewing over what Mama had said. Thoughts rolled through her head on how she could show her.

Shaving my head bald—that would show her.

She hated her hair anyway. She could do it.

Mama would freak. She'd pass out in shock at the first sight of her shiny brown head. Then she'd pass out a second time when she came to.

It sure would be worth seeing.

The problem was, she would freak herself once the initial novelty of it wore off. The idea of looking like Elijah didn't appeal to her. The rock 'n' roller look was just fine for him, but she would just look like a freak. She didn't need to give anyone more of a reason to call her different. And she didn't really hate her hair. Some days she loved it and others she wished for some nice, straight pull-a-brush-through-and-go locks.

And contrary to what Mama seemed to think, Shanice did care about what she looked like—she just didn't care to look like everyone else seemed to think she should. Shanice Ella Stevenson was her own person. Her style wasn't controlled or dictated by teen magazines or television shows. Mama was just going to have to deal with that fact, because Shanice was who she was.

She took off down the street, slicing through the still, humid air.

Sweat beads formed on her upper lip as she raced toward the elementary school yard.

Swimming this afternoon is going to feel good.

The clouds that loomed overhead warned that her plans might not fly, but Shanice hardly paid attention to them. She was just going to worry about skating right now.

The lone elementary school in town sat beside the public library, both three-story brick buildings with engraved inscriptions written in Latin letters above the doors that had long been forgotten. One walkway to the school had four stairs with a metal handrail and a handicap ramp connecting it to the public sidewalk. Living in a town with no designated skater area, the walkway had become a favorite of the handful of skilled skaters.

School officials would rant about liability at the beginning of the school year and even place someone on the premises with the sole purpose of chasing them away when they got there, but the skaters would always outlast them. By the time spring rolled around, they were left unchecked to play around.

She turned the corner to find the walkway empty.

Weird. No one's here at all?

Skating up the ramp, she looked around again. The serious skater group in town was small. Other than herself, Elijah, and Parker, there were a few middle schoolers who had skills. It really wasn't much of a skater-friendly town.

Yet usually someone else was here.

She shrugged and headed toward the stairs, lowering her body for momentum. As she gained speed, she fixed her eyes on the goal ahead: It was a simple jump over the four steps and onto the sidewalk below. Easy as can be. As she reached the top step, her front wheel caught in a small groove momentarily. She lurched forward, trying to grab the handrail for support. She missed. As she spilled down the stairs, her right leg scraped roughly against the rugged edge of the concrete stairs, ripping at her flesh. She cried out in pain as she hit the sidewalk below and ground debris deeper into her wounds. Gravel that had spilled over from the roadside parking lot bit into her leg.

Man, did anyone see that?

In the fifty other times she had successfully made that jump, she had never noticed that hole in the sidewalk before. Of course she would have to hit it when no one else was around. She propped herself up on the bottom step and looked around to see if anyone had witnessed her mishap. No one was around.

Damage assessment time. . .

Wiggling each wrist, she was happy to feel no pain. Inside her skates, her feet felt fine as well. Blood covered the inside of her arm at her elbow. She examined it closely and was relieved to find it to be only another scrape, nothing some good old soap and water couldn't handle. Somehow she had managed to keep her face from hitting anything, so she was fine there.

She turned her attention to the burning sensation on her calf. The entire side of her leg was raw and bloody. The wound's jagged edges were littered with dirt and tiny pieces of gravel. Shanice sighed. Mama was going to make her go to the hospital. Any wound with more surface area than a standard large bandage meant Mama wouldn't mess with it. And when she saw that kind of dirt in it, she would definitely cart Shanice off to the emergency room.

Probably talking the whole time about how unladylike gaping wounds caused by skating spills are.

Again, she looked around, hoping for a familiar face of some kind, but the street was empty.

Looks like you're getting home on your own, sister.

Using the handrail for leverage, she raised herself to her feet. Her leg burned, but she was relieved to realize that the pain was localized to the wound only and didn't run deeper to the bone.

Ha-ha. Another spill, another cheated broken bone. Go, me!

At least congratulating herself made her ego feel a bit better, even if it didn't do anything for the pain in her leg. She moved gingerly, shuffling her feet back and forth as she headed out into the street toward her home. She wanted desperately to spy Parker and Elijah heading for the walkway or, better yet, her home. If she could just lean on someone instead of having to put the strain on her leg muscles, the pain would be bearable. With every movement, her leg screamed.

Gritting her teeth, she prayed silently, asking for strength to get home. Mama could yell at her all she wanted as long as she would help her and hug her when the hospital trip was all done. She'd take all the bad-mouthing in the world about being a tomboy if it meant she got home as quickly and in as little pain as possible.

Slowly, the pain dulled with each stride. The throbbing turned into an ache, and her muscles loosened. Moving became much more bearable. The blood was still seeping in spots on her leg as she entered her driveway. Her arm and the side of her shirt were caked in dry blood and sweat when she reached the porch.

"Hey now," Mama called, still cleaning her strawberries as she heard the sound of wheels on her hardwood floor. Mama was pretty picky about what touched her floor, and skates were definitely not allowed. She turned to scold and gasped at the sight of her only child. "Sit down, baby. Sit down." Her voice became strong and confident. The surety in her voice calmed Shanice instantly.

If Mama thinks it's okay, then it's going to be okay.

Shanice eased herself into a chair and laid her head back in relief.

Mama barked at Tawny to grab the first-aid box from the bathroom down the hallway. Finding a clean towel in the drawer, she wet it down and knelt beside her daughter. "You didn't get hit by a car or anything, did you?" she asked as she dabbed at the scrape on her arm.

Shanice shook her head and closed her eyes as Tawny entered the room. The last thing she needed to see was a smirk on her face.

"Oh, yuck," Jalin said as he entered the room.

"Yuck is right," Mama agreed. The child scrambled back toward the sink and the unguarded berries. "Now don't make your Auntie 'Nay have to whup you, little man. You stay away from those berries."

The boy covered his mouth with his hands and giggled, knowing as well as Shanice did that her mama never "whupped" anyone—especially children who were little and cute like her nephew.

Mama gingerly cleansed the edges of the wound. Shanice opened her eyes to see Tawny sitting on the floor with Mama, eyeing the ugly wound on her leg.

"I don't think I'm going to be able to clean this out on my own," Mama sighed, folding up the blood-stained towel. "I think we're going to need to go to the ER. I just don't want to leave one of those stones in there and see it get infected."

I knew you'd say that. If I would have been closer to the hospital, I would have just told you to meet me there.

She nodded instead, just glad to be home. Surprisingly, Tawny's presence was hardly annoying at all. Checking out the hole in her leg, she saw that it was hardly bleeding anymore except for two places that seemed the deepest. It still stung and burned terribly, and her whole leg felt tingly numb.

Mama looked at Tawny momentarily like she was trying to decide if she should stay home with Jalin or go with them.

Tawny turned and called her brother back into the room. "Come on, Jay-Jay. We have to get going. We need to get Shanice to the hospital to get her all better."

Okay, what gives? You're being nice to me again.

Mama seemed content with not having to play the bad guy role. She gathered up her wireless phone and purse and instructed Tawny to find Jalin's shirt and shoes and meet her in the car.

Shanice pulled herself up again and tried to hobble her way to the door. She was determined to do it alone, but the pain told her otherwise.

Mama cradled her unhurt arm and told her to sit back down. "The skates will tell the doctors all they need to know, but we're going to get them off. No use scuffing up the hospital floors with them. Now how do you unbuckle these things?"

"I'll get it, Mama," Shanice said, wincing as she bent her leg.

"I know how to do it," Tawny volunteered. "They fasten just like mine."

What? Tawny skates?

Her cousin knelt down, straightening Shanice's leg out, and pulled the skates off one by one. "Serious fall, cuz."

Shanice nodded. "On a jump I've done a hundred times."

Tawny helped her up and to the car. Jalin scrambled out the door behind her. "Shay got a boo-boo," he said as he climbed into his car seat.

Shay? That's kind of cool.

As they drove through town, Shanice waited for the inevitable. Mama was sure to start on how dangerous her hobbies were and how they were meant for thrill-seeking boys instead of her daughter. She'd probably even remind her how dainty Tawny was with her manicured nails and perfect bouncy curls. "Tawny would never try such a foolish thing," Mama was sure to say.

That's because Tawny doesn't leave the couch. If she even mentions Tawny's name, I'll just die. So maybe she owns a pair of blades. I bet if Tawny ever does use them, she never even considers jumping a set of stairs. More likely, she got them during one of her dad's guilt-trip shopping sprees. I bet she never even wears them. Why would she, since she watches videos all day? If there is any justice, all that couch sitting is going to catch up to Tawny. We'll see how dainty she is when she weighs nine hundred pounds.

Then maybe Mama would see the benefits to blading and actually doing something physically strenuous. There had to be something *lady-like* about getting off your butt and doing something once in awhile! If a curvy athletic figure didn't make her girly enough, nothing was going to.

Shanice laid her head back against the seat of the car and closed her eyes.

Someday. . .

Tawny led Jalin over to the toy box as they entered the emergency room. The boy squealed with delight at the sight of the mangled pile of junk that vaguely resembled toys. Tawny turned up her nose and tried to direct his attention to a book instead. He wanted nothing to do with it. Diving right into the box, he squealed again.

Shanice found a seat as Mama went to check her in at the front desk. She grimaced at the sight of her little cousin popping a grimy block into his mouth. They were the filthiest toys she had ever seen, especially for being in a hospital.

"How ya doing?" Tawny asked as Shanice leaned back into the chair.

"Still in shock that I fell," she replied honestly. "I've done that jump so many times."

"It sure looks like it hurts."

"Yeah, it does."

Mama thanked the receptionist and scooped up Jalin as she went past. "Those toys are dirty, baby. Come keep Aunt 'Nay warm. This place is cold." Mama always had a way of making even the littlest kid feel important. He curled up on her lap, hugging her tightly.

Tawny picked up a magazine and flipped idly through it. Stopping at a full-page spread of a hip-hop artist, she plopped it in Shanice's lap and said, "Now is that yummy or what?"

Shanice studied the picture. His smiling face was square with a strong chin, yet it still had a babyish quality to it. His eyes were a beautiful deep brown. The white silk T-shirt showed off dark muscled arms crossed in front of him. He *was* cute. And his smile said that he knew it.

"Now that's a man," Tawny stated. "You want a real man? *That's* what you look for. Not anything like those freak-boy runts you hang out with."

Shanice went back to watching Mama. Two-year-old Jalin began to squirm. The picture from the magazine flooded her thoughts as she pondered what Tawny had said.

A real man. Huh?

What made him a "real man"? He was muscled and handsome and, at least in that picture, not some gold-toothed, tattooed thug. Was that what made Tawny say he was a real man? Or was this another race thing she was trying to pull? Was the hip-hop star a "real man" because he was black? Were Parker and Elijah not because they weren't black? Curiosity was getting to her, but she didn't want to start something with her cousin by asking Tawny to explain. Shanice never knew what would set her off, so she opted to keep her musings to herself and wait for the doctors.

Elijah is cute in a pure rock star kind of way, and Parker is just plain adorable. That guy in the picture was in his twenties. Parker will be quite a hunk at that age—full-page spread material himself.

When Shanice was called back, Mama asked her if she should go too. Shanice looked again at her leg. Only one small spot was still bleeding. She assured Mama that she would be okay and that Mama could wait with Tawny and Jalin.

Reaching over to touch her face, Mama smiled and nodded. "You are getting so grown up," she lamented. "If you need anything, I'm right out here."

As she followed the nurse back, Shanice wished Mama had come with her anyway. The smell of hospitals and the sounds of the ER were still a bit overwhelming for her. She had never spent a moment in the patients' area without Mama or Daddy. Sometimes it paid to grow up; other times it did not.

Sitting on the slab the nurse referred to as a bed, Shanice dutifully answered her questions, but her mind was back in the waiting room. Had she and Tawny just had a moment? She went over the events in her head again. They might have had a real conversation had Shanice actually opened her mouth and said something back. Was her cousin just going through one of her mood-swing things, soon to return to her normal mean self, or was she really making an effort to smooth things out?

"Are you ready?" the nurse said again. Shanice sort of remembered hearing her say it the first time. "This is going to hurt a bit even with the local anesthetic I just applied."

Shanice clamped her hands down on the sides of the bed and nodded. She'd had dirt-filled wounds scrubbed out before at the ER. She knew what to expect. And it was absolutely no fun at all.

Biting at her bottom lip, she tried to think of anything but the feeling of the wire brush-like tool the nurse was using on her leg. Her thoughts went back to her cousin and the times they had spent together as children. She missed how Tawny used to see her as a friend—not like this visit during which she was constantly reminded that they were different. They'd had great times together, here and back in Detroit. Back then, nothing but the good times seemed to matter.

"You did a pretty good number on this," the nurse stated as she poured liquid over the scrape.

Shanice nodded, trying to ignore the discomfort it caused. "I was skating and I didn't make the jump."

"In my day, skates were made to keep the wheels on the ground," she said kindly. "I still had plenty of banged-up knees myself. The doctor's going to come in and take a look at this and make sure you don't have any broken bones or anything like that in there."

"Nothing feels broken," Shanice replied. Not that she really knew what something broken felt like.

"Well, I'm sure your mother would prefer him to check it out to be sure."

Shanice nodded again as the nurse closed the curtain around her "room."

"Our God is an awesome God," she started to sing quietly to herself as she scanned the room for something interesting to look at. There was nothing save a poster with different smiley faces indicating how to judge the amount of pain the reader was feeling. They reminded Shanice of computer emoticons. She stared at them, trying to decide which computer keys would be needed to create each one.

You really are bored.

There would be no trip to the pool this afternoon. Though, with her luck, Mama would still make her take Jalin over to the wading pool for at least a little while. She'd be stuck cooking on the deck of the warm two-feet-deep pool instead of having half her body submerged in it.

Her thoughts drifted to her friends and what they were all doing right now. Jenna Rose, the Barbie doll wannabe, was probably brushing her hair and counting the strokes in a very Marcia Brady-like fashion. Darby was bent over a spiral notebook with pure talent showing on the ink-written pages in front of her, yet she would be too shy to show the pages to anyone. Andria was probably hiding in her room, listening to some gothic movie score and doodling Elijah's name on a piece of paper while counting down the days until she could move out of her house. Amber had to be mixing some classic worship tune to some weird music, and the boys were skating somewhere. *Without me.* She wondered if anyone wondered what she was doing right now.

A middle-aged man with plastic-looking hair and a white doctor's coat opened the curtain without warning.

It's a good thing I wasn't naked. He didn't even knock!

But then again, there was no reason for her to be naked, so she supposed there was really no reason for him to knock before entering. It just seemed a little rude of him.

"Hello," he said, looking up her name on the clipboard in his hand.

You could have at least learned my name before barging in. You must be a real hit with the little kids around here.

"Shanice," he added as he found her name. "What do we have here?"

"You're looking at it," she replied. If Mama had been here, Shanice would have gotten it for being rude. Shanice just wasn't in the mood to sugarcoat things for someone who was rude toward her.

The doctor's bedside manner skills were minimal. He went to work, using the wire brush tool a couple more times and examining the wound closely after each rinse. For the rest of the time he was there, he didn't say another word. Checking her ankle, he decided X-rays weren't needed.

Shanice went back to daydreaming about her friends. She wondered if Jenna Rose still had a thing for Parker. Shanice secretly did. It was one of those deep-in-the-recesses-of-your-mind kind of things that only came to the surface when she was in situations like this. Shanice adored Parker, but their friendship was too important to let something as silly as an attraction get in the way. Besides, someone like Jenna Rose was much more his type. When he decided he was done flirting and ready to find his type, he would end up with Jenna Rose or someone just like her.

But those eyes of Parker's. . .that was plenty to think about and pass the time. Any girl who didn't get lost in those baby blues had some serious issues.

Someone at church camp once told her that there was an advantage to being biracial—you weren't bound by society's views of who was acceptable to date.

She wondered how true that really was.

Not that Shanice would have cared anyway. She was used to living by what God said was acceptable, and not once did He ever make skin color an issue. If He wasn't going to make it an issue, neither was she.

Mama had found her perfect man in a skinny, blond white boy studying to be a teacher, and despite the disapproval she received from most of her family and the black community in general, she married him. Together they had made a life that had to be very pleasing in God's eyes.

"Well," the doctor said, pulling off his gloves, "the nurse will be back in to dress that for you and you'll be free to go. Is your mom outside in the waiting room?"

She nodded, alarmed at the fact that he would ask. Something must be wrong for him to do that.

"We're going to need to discuss with her how to keep this clean for the next few days. You have one nasty hole in your leg there, and it's going to take some special care. And it looks like that ankle is sprained. I'll send the nurse out to ask your mom back." He cradled the clipboard in his arm and disappeared through the curtain.

A few seconds later, Mama scurried in. "What's going on? Something broken?"

"Nope," Shanice replied, scooting over to make room for Mama. Mama took her hand and sat down on the side of the bed. "At least I don't think so. He said something about instructing you on how to keep it clean over the next few days or something."

"That's weird," she mumbled. "I know how to keep a scrape clean."

A short, frumpy nurse entered the room holding the clipboard. She smiled at Shanice as she entered and went about gathering up gauze pads and medical tape. "I'm sorry, sweetie," she said, "but this is not going to be pleasant for you for the next few days." She dabbed the liquid again on the wound and folded up one of the pads. "Mrs. Stevenson, I need to show you how to care for this." The nurse pointed to the area of her leg where the hole was the deepest. "We have to watch this area in particular."

The nurse went about packing the hole with the folded gauze and laying a large piece of gauze over the entire wound. She taped it in place and patted Shanice on the other knee. "Okay," she said, "that's the easy part." She turned her attention back to Mama. "Three times a day you need to pull this off, cleanse it, and rebandage it the same way. For the next five days. It's going to hurt, but you need to get the bandage off as quickly and cleanly as possible each time. We need to lift up as many of the dead cells as possible out of that hole each time so it can heal properly."

Mama took her daughter's hand and squeezed it. "It will hurt?" she asked.

The nurse nodded. "But it has to be done or it's going to get infected. I know it doesn't sound pleasant, but you have to do it. The ankle is sprained as well, so she has to stay off it for a few weeks."

Shanice closed her eyes. If a nurse said something like that, it wasn't going to be pretty at all. Most of the time they tried to sugarcoat stuff. The nurse left the room to gather up their discharge papers.

Mama wrapped an arm around her daughter's shoulder and tried to smile.

Shanice shook her head, glad to feel her mama's embrace. She hadn't shown Shanice much affection in the past few days, and it felt good to have a few moments alone with just the two of them.

The nurse returned and soon they were on their way out the door. In the waiting room, Tawny sat in the same chair, only now her two-year-old brother was asleep on her shoulder. When she saw them enter the room, she smiled.

Wow. Was that another moment?

"Very becoming," she giggled, hefting her brother to her hip as she stood up. "Looks like your skating days are about over."

Just on hold, cuz. Just on hold. It'd be like asking you if you were going to stop curling your hair after a bad hair day. Of course I'm still going to skate.

Shanice shrugged her shoulders as she hobbled through the room on her crutches. The pain was just a slight sting now, but the stiffness in her leg made it awkward to walk. "I'll be back in no time."

The late afternoon sun beat down mercilessly as they left the air-conditioned building. A haze hung in the still, humid air. Shanice's dad loved days like this—thunderstorms were bound to appear before the night arrived.

They hurried to the car and headed home.

"Well," Mama said, "we're late for the salon now. I think we're just going to head straight over there and see if they can get us in."

Shanice groaned. "Can you take me to Angelino's then, Mama? We have practice in about an hour."

Mama looked at her watch and stared straight ahead as she pulled the car from the parking lot. Shanice knew Mama didn't take their band too seriously. She just didn't seem to have their vision. Small-town people weren't supposed to do big things in Mama's eyes. Of course, living in one of the big cities would have its advantages, but as far as God's will was concerned, Shanice knew it made no difference where a person came from. Mama thought her daughter was talented, and certainly she was proud of her, but she just didn't get it completely.

"What kind of practice?" Tawny asked from the backseat.

Shanice's heart sank. Tawny was going to ask to come too. And Mama was going to make Shanice take her or she wouldn't let her daughter go.

The salon was her last hope.

"Shanice and her friends have a band," Mama replied. "They tinker around and seem to have a good time with it."

"It's more than 'tinkering,' Mama," Shanice retorted. "We've had real gigs and everything, and we have another one coming up, so I have to be there. Can't we reschedule the salon trip?"

"What do you want to do, Tonya?" Mama asked as they came to a halt at a stop sign. "Do you want to do the salon today or would you like to go with Shanice?"

Go to the salon. Go to the salon.

"I think I'll go with Shanice."

CHAPTER 14

Dreading what was about to come, Shanice held open the door to the pizza shop for her cousin. A table of patrons looked up as they entered the small dining area before quickly returning to their meal. Tawny waited for Shanice to hobble through the door on her crutches.

"Haven't they ever seen black people?" Tawny whispered over her cousin's shoulder.

Shanice elbowed her in reply.

Mrs. Angelino appeared from behind the counter and threw open her arms. "Shanice!" she greeted her with a firm hug. "We've missed your voice around here the past few days. I don't like the summer months too well. You kids keep me company more than you know."

Hugging her back, Shanice smiled. "We need to practice more than we have been if we plan on going anywhere with this. Chance went to the beach for a week and we all got lazy." She turned her attention to her cousin, who was examining a picture on the wall. "Mrs. Angelino, this is my cousin Tawny."

"Hello, my dear." Mrs. Angelino gasped as she suddenly noticed the bandage on Shanice's leg. "Oh, what in the world happened? Are you okay?"

Shanice nodded. "I'm fine. I just fell and scraped up my leg and sprained my ankle."

"Bad enough to go to the hospital," Tawny added.

"Do you need to sit down?"

Shanice giggled. All this attention was going to be nice. She'd have to milk it for as long as she could. "No, ma'am. I'm fine, really. It's just a big scrape and my leg is pretty stiff. No big deal."

Seemingly satisfied, the round Italian woman wrapped her arms around the newcomer and squeezed her tightly. Shanice had to stop herself from laughing at the baffled look on her cousin's face. "Any cousin of Shanice's is a friend of mine," Mrs. Angelino said warmly. "What would you girls like to drink?"

A customer walked to the counter behind them.

"I'll get it," Shanice offered. "Thank you. We'll get out of your way."

Filling their glasses, Shanice watched her cousin grab a seat in a booth by the window. She sat quietly and gazed out over the parking lot. A booth wasn't going to be enough room for everyone when they got there.

I wonder what must be going through her head.

Maybe she was finally taking the right steps to find out a little of what Tawny was thinking. Maybe it was a good thing Tawny had come with her. Or maybe this was going to be a serious disaster. Either way, they were already here, and the rest of the gang was probably on their way. Sink or swim, Tawny was finally going to meet the rest of her friends.

And probably even worse, her friends were finally going to meet her cousin.

As she set down the glasses in front of them, Tawny turned her attention to her cousin. "So how's it feel?"

Why are you being nice to me all of a sudden?

Shanice eased her way into the booth, the skin on her leg feeling like a board. It refused to give as she tried to bend her knee a bit. "I've been better, I'll say that much."

Twirling her straw thoughtfully, Tawny stared at the ice cubes as they floated around in her soda. "Tell me about this band thing."

Watching the door for any sign of her friends, Shanice tried to think of what to say. Tawny was a homegirl through and through. She didn't get into rock music, and she was sure to crack on her cousin for being into it.

"Well, tell me," Tawny insisted, taking a sip from the straw and resting her arms on the table.

"It's just a group of my friends," Shanice began, trying to downplay things. "We're all really into music and we get together to play. It just went from there."

"That's sweet," her cousin replied, genuine admiration sounding in her voice. "You made it sound more serious talking to your mama about it. What do you play?"

"I do vocals."

"Well, you always could sing."

Trying to hide her surprise, Shanice gulped down the last of her soda. Not only was her cousin being nice to her all of a sudden, but she was complimenting her too. What was up with this?

Parker and Elijah burst through the door, laughing loudly, their guitar cases in hand. Waving at the sight of the two girls, Elijah walked over and scooted into the bench beside Shanice. Parker gave him a quick look and sat on the edge of the bench beside Tawny. Shanice flashed him a smile, hoping he would catch that it was all right. For the moment at least, Tawny wasn't going to bite off his head or anything.

He smiled back nervously. "So, Tawny, right?" he asked.

"Yeah," Shanice replied. "You remember my friends, Elijah and Parker."

Tawny nodded and took another drink of her soda. She didn't look too thrilled.

"Elijah plays bass, and Parker does rhythm guitar."

"Came to hang out with us?" Elijah asked, slurping down what was left of Shanice's drink.

Shrugging her shoulders, Tawny made a face like she had no choice and nodded. "What else do I have to do?"

The silence was awkward as they each shifted in their seats, momentarily unsure of what to say next. Shanice now knew what that friendship-killing silence was like. She had never felt it before, and she didn't want to experience it any longer.

"I'm hungry," Parker broke in. "Tawny, what kind of pizza do you like? We got here early to eat, and I'm eating."

Tawny thought for a moment and then said, "Oh, I'm not hungry."

"Sure you are," he insisted.

Shanice tried not to roll her eyes as she looked out the window. Not hungry, please. She had to be starving after spending most of the day at the emergency room. She didn't know if Tawny was trying to be a little priss or what, but she knew that her cousin loved pizza and would gladly eat several slices if it were in front of her. "You still like veggie and cheese?" she asked.

"Whatever is fine," she replied.

Parker took their glasses and headed to the counter. He turned around and held up Tawny's glass. "What are you drinking?" he called.

"It's diet," she replied. "Thanks."

Parker got his hug from Mrs. Angelino and ordered their pizza. Shanice smiled as she watched him interact with the two elderly Italians.

Tawny's smirk caught her attention.

"What?" she asked.

"Please," Tawny replied, turning her attention back to the window. Her usual foul mood was slowly creeping back around.

Embarrassed, Shanice looked away quickly, glad that her complexion easily hid her reddened face.

Okay, sue me. He's not a twenty-year-old thug, but he's beautiful and he's a sweetheart. . .and a man of God. I would think that makes him more of a "man" than your rapping guy.

Parker returned carrying four teetering glasses on a tray. He passed out the drinks and took his seat again.

"Hey," Elijah said, "want a job? You do a pretty good job of that."

"Would you be my boss?"

"Sure would."

"Then I think I'll pass," Parker replied. He put the end of his straw in his mouth and shot the rest of the wrapper at Shanice. She swatted at the projectile but missed as it lodged in her hair.

"You work here?" Tawny asked Elijah.

He nodded. "My aunt and uncle own the place. I help them out."

"Get paid for it?"

Shanice wasn't sure why she was so interested in Elijah all of a sudden. Actually, it made her a bit uncomfortable. Tawny always had an agenda. Watching her intently for some sign of what she was after, Shanice fished the paper out of her braids. Tawny noticed her gaze and smiled, raising her eyebrows mischievously.

Why?" Elijah asked. "You looking for a job?"

Tawny took a long drink of her soda. "Yeah, I might be. What else do I have to do?"

"She's only going to be here for the summer," Shanice added.

"We could probably use some help for the summer," Elijah said.

She cannot work in my sanctuary. I didn't even want her to come this time. I definitely do not want her working here all the time.

"I'll have to check with Aunt 'Nay, but I don't think she'd have a problem. Do you think?" she asked Shanice.

She shrugged her shoulders in response.

"It'd be cool to have some cash," Tawny lamented as Mrs. Angelino appeared with their dishes and silverware.

Cash for what? To sit and count as you watch videos on my couch all day?

Shanice rolled her eyes and stirred her drink with her straw. Like Tawny needed a job. . .

"You looking for a job?" the elderly woman asked as she laid out their silverware in front of them.

"She might be," her nephew replied.

"Can you outwork him?"

Tawny smiled, embarrassed, and hid her face.

"It wouldn't be hard," Parker said, kicking his friend under the table.

"Well," Mrs. Angelino said with a smile, "your pizzas are just about done. You need to hurry up and eat and get to singing. I miss that music."

Ding. The bell rang cheerfully as the door swung open. The twins walked through along with a family of patrons. Darby, dressed in black pants and a body-skimming dark purple shirt, clutched her notebook with one hand and held a soft-shelled guitar case in the other. Her sister followed in a pair of black cutoffs, a black tee with a silver star on the front, and pink Chuck Taylors.

They gathered up a couple chairs and found a place around the booth.

Shanice watched her friends, noting that neither one had said a word since entering. She tried to catch either one's attention, but they both were drawn into their own little worlds.

I wonder what happened while I was at the hospital.

"Where have you been hiding all day?" Parker asked, turning toward Shanice.

"Busy," she replied. She was a bit surprised that no one had noticed her bandaged leg even though the table mostly hid it. They also hadn't noticed the pair of crutches leaning against their table. Parker had bumped her leg a couple of times since he'd been there, but the pain had hardly been noticeable.

"She bit it," Tawny answered for her. "We spent the day in the hospital."

Everyone listened intently as Shanice told the story again.

Amber walked over in the middle of it. Andria shared half of her chair so they could all squeeze around the booth.

"I can't believe you missed that jump," Elijah laughed.

"Thanks for caring about how I'm doing!" Shanice exclaimed. "I'm glad to see who my friends are. And why weren't you out there in the first place? You two, like, never miss a day to skate."

Parker patted his guitar case. "We went over to the music shop to get new strings on my guitar."

"You shoulda called," Elijah added. "We would have been there."

Mr. Angelino appeared with the two pizzas and put them on the table. He rubbed his nephew's fuzzy head playfully. "So I hear someone here is interested in a job. If you work harder than the boy here, I have a job for you."

"Doesn't take much," he added as he patted Elijah's shoulder.

Shanice rested her chin on her hand and watched Elijah's face fall as his uncle looked away. Obviously, her friend didn't find it as humorous as did Mr. Angelino.

Look at you, 'Nice! You're like "Miss Sensitive" all of a sudden. What's this all about?

She knew there was nothing wrong with being concerned about the welfare of her friends. But the new, observant writer side of her had brought all kinds of new thoughts to her head, and she rather liked it.

As she scanned the faces of her friends, she saw a plethora of hurts and problems. Elijah's parents were so messed up that the Angelinos were his guardians, and he seldom visited his parents. Parker was too afraid to tell his stepdad that he even attended church, and the twins' home was a ticking time bomb. Amber's mom and dad lived on separate coasts and refused even to be in the same room together on their daughter's birthday. No one knew what had happened with Jenna Rose's mom, but they gathered that she must not be alive anymore based on the way Jenna Rose talked about her—or mostly didn't talk about her. Yet that's what Shanice loved about them all. No matter what they were going through, they were there for one another. And even though their lives weren't perfect, they didn't punish Shanice for the fact that her home was very much like a *Brady Bunch* episode.

Why had she been so worried about how Tawny would take to her friends? She fit in with these people better than Shanice did. She looked at her cousin, waiting for her to answer the man. She was staring back out the window again. "My cousin Tawny was thinking about getting a job while she's here, Mr. Angelino," Shanice answered.

Tawny turned and nodded at him.

"Any cousin of yours would be more than welcome on my staff," he replied. "I could use an extra pair of hands. We always get busier in the summer." He held out his hand for a handshake. Tawny grasped it and smiled. "You can come in tomorrow to fill out some papers and get started." He passed a smile around the table to everyone and told them to enjoy the pizza as he walked away.

Darby led a prayer before handing out slices of the warm pizza. They giggled and talked as they munched on the food. Shanice continued to watch her friends as they tried to get to know her cousin more. Tawny would have none of it—the good mood that brought her here had vanished.

Just don't start calling people racist or something, cuz.

Then again, her cousin seemed to save the race cracks only for her listening enjoyment.

As they finished up their meal, the conversation turned to the gig coming up in a couple days.

"I think we should play something new in the set," Andria said, elbowing her sister. "Darb's got some great stuff, and I think it's time for us to start showcasing it."

Darby shook her head. "I don't think I have anything good enough for that."

"Yes, you do," her sister argued. "Your stuff is as good as anything we do. And between Jenna Rose and Shanice here, we have the singers to pull anything off."

On cue, Jenna Rose entered the room. She hurried over, apologizing for being late. Andria grabbed up the last piece of veggie pizza and plopped it on a plate for her friend. Jenna Rose thanked her as she pulled up another chair.

"She sings too?" Tawny asked her cousin, eyeing the newcomer.

Shanice bobbed her head up and down enthusiastically. "Oh, does she ever. That girl has *the* voice."

Tawny looked the blond up and down again. "I bet I know who's the lead," she mumbled to herself. Shanice bit her lip and gave Tawny a dirty look. If Tawny was going to cause something, Shanice knew it would be over Jenna Rose. Her cousin's attitude was rather predictable. Fortunately, no one else at the table heard Tawny.

"Come on, Jenna," Parker picked at her, "scarf that pizza down so we can get busy."

Elijah cut in, still wanting to discuss the topic of the band and the upcoming gig. "Do we have anything to music yet that we can do, Darb?"

Again, Darby shook her head. "I just don't know if any of them are good enough."

Parker reached across the table and took his friend's hand in his. "Darby, they are good. They are really good. You were blessed with a talent, and God wants you to put it to use. Those lyrics aren't doing anyone any good hiding in your notebook."

With her hand firmly covering the spiral-bound notebook, Darby stared at its red cover in thought. At last she said slowly, "I've put one to piano, but I haven't even thought of the accompaniment yet. Plus, we don't even have a keyboard in the group."

"We can fix that," Elijah replied. "Most of the places we play have pianos, and we'll just have to get our hands on a keyboard. You and Parker both play piano, right?"

Parker agreed emphatically. "If we need it, Darb, we'll get it somehow. We have the demo session the last week of July to shoot for. I would really love to see at least two original songs on it."

"We have to," Amber added. "My dad says that the formula for a good demo is a couple of remakes that showcase the singers' abilities and a couple of new songs to show off the group's writing ability—"

"Or lack thereof," Darby interrupted.

"Oh, be quiet," Jenna Rose instructed.

"The new songs need to show your writing ability and the band's ability," Amber continued. "It's always important to have a good mix of both. Showing off Jenna's voice isn't going to be difficult."

"Yeah," Parker said, smiling at Jenna Rose as she dropped her pizza crust on the plate, "it pretty much shows itself off."

Shanice caught Tawny smirking again out of the corner of her eye. She'd think differently when she heard Jenna Rose's voice. No matter what her problem was with Jenna Rose's Malibu Barbie appearance, even Tawny couldn't deny a voice like hers.

Elijah reached over and patted Darby's arm. "We need to work on Saturday's set tonight and get it down. Starting Monday, we'll work on writing some music to your lyrics."

"I still don't think they're good enough," she whispered.

"Well," he replied, "that's what we're here for. To make them better."

Andria hugged her sister tightly and jumped to her feet. "So, are we ready to go make some music or what?"

CHAAPTER 115

Tawny, with her normal exaggerated reluctance, picked up her glass and followed them into the back room of the pizza shop. A silver drum set took up one corner of the tiny stage, and microphones and amplifiers were clustered all around it. Two tables in the opposite corner offered seating, and another table was covered with sheets of paper and a box. The wire shelving that lined the opposite wall was empty. Amber's mixing board was beside the door they entered. The musty smell of old cardboard hung in the air.

"You don't play to very big crowds, do you?" Tawny asked her cousin as they watched the others get their instruments ready. Darby climbed onto her bar stool with her acoustic guitar slung over her arm, and her sister sat behind the drums.

Shanice rolled her eyes. "This is just our practice room. We get people in here now and then, but we don't play to a real audience in here."

"It's a good thing," she replied, finding a seat. "How long are we going to be here?"

"We haven't even started yet, Tawny. We'll be awhile," she answered, throwing her hands up in the air. "It's called 'practice' for a reason. Call Mama if you want to go home."

"That's probably what you want, huh?"

"Grow up," Shanice sighed as she turned to join the others.

Jenna Rose tinkered with her microphone stand and grinned at

Shanice as she turned on her own microphone. "She seems fun," she whispered.

"Loads of it," came the reply.

"Let's play it straight through the first time and see what Tawny thinks about it," Parker said.

For the next hour, they played their set—a mix of upbeat Christian rock songs and well-known, heavy-on-the-guitar worship music. Jenna Rose was on fire as usual. Shanice loved to sing, but she could listen to her friend sing all day. Jenna Rose's voice was powerful and absolutely pitch-perfect. Though proud of her own voice, Shanice knew that a gift like her friend's didn't come around often, and they were blessed to have her in their group.

Tawny looked as bored as she could while the band played. Shanice tried to ignore her, but the more she attempted it, the more she was drawn to watching her cousin. Tawny was driving her nuts with her staring at the ceiling and laying her head on the table.

Why does she have to be so rude? Then again, at least she's not yelling obscenities or something at everyone. Count your blessings.

As Darby finished up the chords on the last song, Parker unplugged his guitar and rushed to Tawny's table. "So what'd ya think?" he asked.

Shanice went about putting the microphones into their travel tote, watching her cousin intently for a response. At the first sign of real trouble, she planned to cart Tawny home.

Tawny shook her head and hid her face in her hand, faking embarrassment. She looked up at him with a big smile.

What's that, cuz? Flirting with the white boy, are we? I thought he wasn't a real man.

"I don't know," Tawny said as her smile grew wider and she tilted her head to the side. Her perfect, bouncy curls fell to one side of her face, and her eyes sparkled like they did earlier when she was looking at the magazine and daydreaming about the rap star.

"I don't know?" Parker mimicked, always one to get involved in a good flirty conversation. He leaned forward on the chair opposite

Tawny. "Whatcha mean? Did we sound good or not?"

"It's just not my kind of music."

"Man," Shanice called out, finally annoyed with Tawny to the point of getting angry, "just tell us how it sounded, Tawny."

Turning her eyes toward Shanice without moving her head, Tawny smacked her lips loudly. "I was about to get to that, cuz. Quit trippin'."

Shanice turned her back on the scene and pretended to fiddle with her mike amplifier. Andria smiled at her, and she rolled her eyes in return.

"You liked it?" Parker pressed for her answer.

"You guys can play, I guess," Tawny admitted, "but it still wasn't my thing."

"You gonna come see us Saturday?"

"I don't know. Maybe I'll be working then." She tossed her head back, her short hair flipping to the other side of her face. Her eyes were glued to Parker's.

"With any luck," murmured Shanice under her breath. Jenna Rose looked at her and smiled.

Tawny tossed Shanice a dirty look and smiled at Parker again. "But then again, maybe I'll ask for that day off."

Shanice turned her attention to the playlist and tried to pretend her cousin wasn't there. Why she acted like that, Shanice didn't know. She should have insisted Tawny go to the salon and hang out with the "Amen Sisters" where she would have fit in instead of coming down here to make a mockery out of Shanice's friends and what they loved to do together as a band.

"What'd you think, Amber?" Elijah asked. "Did we get it?"

Amber nodded. "I think you guys sounded great."

"Well, I gotta go," Parker said in a hurry. "I didn't realize we got started this late. I need to get home. We're going to meet tomorrow again, right? And, 'Nice, you bringing your cousin again?"

"Not if I can help it," Shanice replied honestly.

Tawny threw her another look. "If you'll be here," she said to Parker, "I might find a reason to come over again."

"I'll definitely be here," he replied, flashing his trademark grin.

You idiot, stop flirting with her. You're only making it all worse. She's not really interested in you, so you might as well forget it.

Shanice knew that Parker had vowed to stop casually dating when he came to know Christ the summer before, and she respected him for that. It had to be hard for such a flirtatious guy to give up that girl-to-girl lifestyle he had been famous for before meeting Darby. Yet sometimes he seemed to forget his own vow and jump right back into it. This whole episode with Tawny seemed to be one of those times.

"Chance'll be back tomorrow," Andria said, handing Parker a couple fliers announcing their gig on Saturday. "Get these up places."

Shanice took a stack of the flyers and punched Parker in the arm as he went by.

"Watch yourself, gimpy," he teased. "Don't make me hurt you."

"I could still take you with one bad leg," she replied.

" 'Nice," her cousin called, standing up from the table, "be a girl just once, will ya?"

With an exasperated sigh, Shanice headed for the door. She was done. She wasn't taking another word from Tawny. The dining room was empty, and Mrs. Angelino was scrubbing down an extremely food-covered table. A high chair nearby was caked with pizza sauce.

"Where are you off to in such a hurry, *mi amore?*" she asked as Shanice burst through the room.

"I just need to go, Mrs. Angelino," Shanice replied. She hesitated at the door. Tawny wouldn't know how to get home. No matter how much she might want to, she couldn't just leave her here.

But everyone in this building knows how to get her home. Go.

Mama would be furious if she left Tawny, Shanice knew. Second Rate would be minus its backup singer, and their group would be minus one friend because Mama would have her head.

"I think if you take off like that your problems are just going to follow you," Mrs. Angelino mused, examining her now-clean tablecloth. "I don't think running will solve anything."

At least it would keep me from killing her. . . .

Darby opened the door from the back room and poked her head out. "Everything okay?" she asked.

Shanice hobbled to the corner, grabbed the broom, and attempted to sweep the floor around where the high chair sat. Her sweeping was sloppy and grew more and more so as she heard Tawny's laughter through the open door.

Darby closed the door and walked over to her friend. " 'Nice, obviously everything is not okay." She eyed the door as Jenna Rose's laugh joined Tawny's. "Is she getting to you?"

Focusing on the sweeping charade, Shanice limped to the next table. She didn't even know what to say without sounding selfish. It was more than Tawny flirting with Parker. In her own little sneaky, manipulative way, Tawny was making fun of everything that Shanice held dear. And it was too much to take to watch Tawny laughing at the people she cared about.

Tawny laughed again.

She was in there making fun of them to their very own faces, and they didn't even realize she was doing it. When she wasn't acting angry or bored, she just made everything seem so innocently funny—like she was just having a good time.

"Tawny seems like she always did," Darby said.

"She's nothing like she used to be," Shanice replied. "She's mean and spiteful and taking over everything important to me."

Darby sat down at a table and scanned her friend's expression. Finally, she spoke. "I think you might be reading a little further into this than you should, 'Nice."

"No," she replied, leaning on the broom. "Believe me, I'm not. Are you ready to go home? Because I am."

"I'll go gather everyone up," Darby answered.

Shanice watched her friends exit the room one at a time. All were laughing and joking, and her cousin was in the middle and giggling right along with them. The pain was returning in her leg, but Shanice was determined to walk home with them. Tawny wasn't taking over her friends.

Not without a fight.

Tawny walked over and wrapped an arm around her cousin's shoulder as the boys left the pizza shop. Parker turned around and waved two fingers, his sweetest smile spread across his face.

"Man," she said, "it's too bad that boy ain't black."

Shanice turned to face her. "What's that got to do with anything?"

"Girl, it's got *everything* to do with everything."

Tawny walked ahead with Darby as Shanice and Andria took a slower pace. Shanice could hear them talking about the last time Tawny had visited. The four of them had spent the summer in the park swimming, playing tennis and basketball, and daydreaming about the boys who crossed their paths. At twelve, they were starting to notice boys but still had no real idea why. It had been a good summer.

"You aren't having fun with her this time, are you?" Andria asked quietly.

Shanice shook her head. "It wouldn't be so bad if she wasn't so nasty. She's picking at me for everything."

"Welcome to the world of having siblings, woman," Andria smirked, trying to lighten up the mood.

Biting her lip, Shanice looked straight ahead as she leaned into her crutches and walked. Andria didn't understand either. This was more than sibling rivalry—Tawny was just plain mean. But how could Andria really understand?

When people look at Tawny, they see a girl. When they look at me, they want to know what I am. There isn't that question hanging over Tawny's head all the time. Like I'm something more than just a girl. Maybe that's Tawny's problem too. . . . She wants to know what she's looking at when she looks at me.

"But what's your problem with her, 'Nice? What's she doing?" Andria asked.

"Nothing," she mumbled. "I guess it's all me."

They walked the rest of the way home in silence. Her leg ached, and she wished that Mama had picked them up instead of them trudging the six blocks home. She knew she should have sucked it in and called Mama to come get them instead of insisting on doing things for herself. By the time the painkillers wore off completely, she was going to be hurting badly. She could feel the pain intensify as she moved.

With her thumbs hooked in the back pockets of her cutoffs, Andria slowed her pace. The way she kept glancing over at Shanice made her nervous. She wasn't used to being the one with the problems. She was a fixer and didn't usually look to others for help in her own time of need.

You're such a baby. Like this is a real "time of need." Grow up and realize that you are going to be seen as different and learn to deal with it.

Andria also seemed uneasy with the role reversal. The way she kept looking at her told Shanice that she didn't know what to say or what Shanice wanted from her. It was a silent message that said *I'm here even though I don't know what I can do to make things better.* If Andria only knew how many times in their lives Shanice had felt that same way toward her. . . .

A strong blast of air hit the girls, bringing with it the sweet aroma of a summer storm. All four sets of eyes studied the darkening sky. Thunder rumbled in the distance as tiny droplets of water plinked off a nearby shed's tin roof. The trees overhead bent and groaned in the force of the wind.

"I think we're going to get—" Before Andria could get the last word out, the skies opened up and the rain poured down in large, loud drops.

Shanice surprised even herself with how fast she and her crutches caught up with Tawny and Darby as the fat, cold drops hit her. Darby turned and kicked her foot through the puddle that had formed on the sidewalk, spraying the others. Her sister splashed back. Holding up her hands in disbelief, Tawny cursed and then began laughing.

"I would say 'Let's run,'" Darby commented, "but it wouldn't get us any drier."

Thunder rolled again in the distance.

"I can't tell if that's getting closer or farther away," Andria said as she turned her face into the rain.

Shanice also turned her face upward, wanting to keep the water from running its sweat-tinted streams into her eyes. She sighed. After such a miserably hot day, even the slight sting from the force of the drops was refreshing.

"I don't think we should stand around to find out," Tawny replied. "How much farther do we have to go?"

"Three blocks," Shanice replied.

Andria darted into a nearby yard. "We can cut it down to two by going through these yards."

The other three followed as they crossed through the backyard of a two-story blue house. The rain continued to pound down on them as they jumped a flower bed and moved into the next lawn. A yappy little dog darted across the yard with them, making Tawny screech. It jumped at her heels, its tail wagging excitedly.

"Go away, little ankle biter," she called through her laughter. "Get out of the rain."

The dog followed, happily joining in their dash until they reached the end of his yard.

"Watch out, Tawn," Andria laughed. "He might bite a toe off."

"I'm not scared of him," she replied. "Back in my neighborhood, it'd be a rottie chasing us!"

A tall wooden fence loomed ahead.

Shanice waved her friends down a driveway back toward the street. Rain continued to beat down on them mercilessly as another rumble of thunder sounded in the distance. The McKennitt house was straight ahead. They could see its green-slated roof through the swaying treetops.

"That was a better shortcut than I thought," Andria laughed as water streamed down her face. With a blow, she sent tiny droplets back into the air. Her sister splashed in a puddle again.

Closing in on home, the friends laughed and danced in the rain.

Shanice hopped around, allowing her frustration to drain away with the streams of water. No thunder could be heard as the rain slowly began to taper into a drizzle.

"I didn't think you could move so fast," Andria giggled, pushing Shanice lightly. "Being all gimpy and everything."

"*I* didn't think I could move so fast," she replied. "I hate thunderstorms, and with my luck today, I'd be the one to get hit by lightning."

Andria dropped backward, falling onto her own soft wet lawn. She looked up at the others as they stared at her quizzically. "I can't get any wetter," she answered.

Darby and Shanice glanced at each other and smiled. They dropped onto the ground beside her.

"Y'all are crazy," her cousin laughed. "You really are. I'm going in the house before I get struck down by lightning. Lying in someone's yard like that—where I'm from, you're liable to get shot doing stuff like that."

Andria and Shanice exchanged glances and reached up together, grabbing Tawny's hands. With one pull, they brought her to the ground between them.

"You can't get any wetter," Shanice repeated her friend's words.

"I don't want to be hit by lightning!"

As if on cue, thunder boomed overhead—this time closer.

"Point taken," Darby said, scrambling to her feet.

"Come on," Shanice directed, leading them across the yard to her house. "Everybody back to my house."

They scrambled through the back door, slamming it in their wake. Mama sat at the kitchen table flipping through a catalog. She closed it quickly and chuckled at the sight of the soaking-wet girls. "Is it raining out there?" she teased.

"Mama, I need a hug," Shanice snickered, opening her arms wide and wrapping them around her mother. "I love you."

Mama shook her head, laughing as she shook the water off her arms. Her shirt was now nearly as wet as Shanice's. "You little brat, I love you too," she replied. "Now go get your friends some towels and dry clothes.

I can't believe you walked home in the storm with that leg, Shanice. You should have called me."

"It caught us off guard," her daughter shrugged.

"We should probably head home," Darby said. "Mom is leaving for the airport first thing in the morning, and I think she wanted to watch a movie together or something tonight. Girl bonding thing. You know the drill."

"Is your daddy leaving town too?" Mama asked, her maternal instincts kicking in full force. Shanice could envision the worries churning away behind her mama's dark eyes.

"Not until Monday," Andria replied. "Mom comes home Wednesday."

"You need anything—day or night—you know where to find me. Even before your daddy leaves. You know I'm always here for you."

Darby nodded appreciatively. Mama patted her on the shoulder as they passed by. The twins said good-bye and left.

"We have severe weather advisories for the rest of the evening, so go get yourselves dried up and plan to hang out at home for the rest of the night, ladies," Mama stated, opening her catalog again. She watched the twins cross in front of the large window that spanned the backyard. "Poor babies."

She paused. "Maybe we'll do a movie and pizza ourselves."

Shanice and Tawny looked at one another and groaned. "How about we do Chinese instead?" Shanice asked.

"I'm not even hungry," Tawny whined, holding her stomach.

"You finally sick of pizza?" Mama asked.

"No," Shanice laughed. "It just doesn't sound as good when you have to pay for it, I guess."

"Those Angelinos, bless their souls," Mama said, shaking her head. "They'd be the richest people in town if they'd stop feeding you kids. You bunch of mooches. Y'all should be ashamed of yourselves."

"Well, I need dry clothes," Tawny said. "I'm freezing."

Mama watched her niece disappear up the stairs. When the girl was out of sight, she turned to her daughter. "I'm glad to see the two of you getting along so well."

"I don't know if that's the case or if we're just tolerating each other," Shanice replied. "We got drenched. It made it pretty easy to laugh and forget about stuff for awhile as we tried to outrun the thunderstorm."

"Well," Mama replied, turning her attention back to the catalog pages, "don't go remembering things too quickly. I'm about to ship the two of you off to church camp or something for the rest of the summer if you don't get along better real soon."

Shanice headed for the stairs. "Yeah, yeah, Mama," she mumbled.

She hobbled up the stairs, went to her room, and changed her clothes.

Tawny was in the hallway as Shanice left her room. A grin spread across her face as she made her way to the bathroom. "Hey, Shanice," she called as her cousin started back down the stairs. "How 'bout you get that weave out and let me braid your hair while we watch that movie?"

"Shoot," Shanice whistled. "That's never been a weave, girl. That's my hair."

"Uh-huh," came the remark through a smile. "I bet it is."

Shanice smiled back, happy at the chance to finally get in a jab at her cousin. "You're just jealous because I can actually grow hair."

"Oh, so now you got jokes?"

Shanice shrugged her shoulders and continued down the stairs.

Tawny came to the top of the steps and watched her slow progress. With a laugh, the girl called out to her cousin, "I'm gonna make you black yet—you watch and see."

CHAPTER 17

Girl movies?" Daddy asked, motioning for the groggy two year old to follow him upstairs. "I think I'll head to bed myself then. I'll watch a good shoot-em-up man flick with Jalin or something in our room."

Mama giggled and reached up on her tiptoes to kiss him. He wrapped his arms around her waist and lifted her into the air. "Good night," she said.

Holding her in the air, he smiled.

Shanice grinned as well. The amount of affection her parents showed toward one another always made her happy. Sometimes they were as bad as teenagers, the way they always had to hold hands in public and steal little kisses and such, but even though Shanice would say she was embarrassed by them, she really loved every minute of it. There was a certain amount of comfort in knowing that her parents were still in love after so many years together. She only wished more of the people she knew had those types of role models in their lives.

Tawny picked up her little brother and held him close. She pretended to be interested in a commercial on television, but Shanice could see the sadness in her eyes. She wondered if Tawny had ever gotten to see that kind of real affection displayed between her parents. And poor baby Jalin—he had probably never witnessed it before. What kind of man was he going to grow up to be without seeing each day how a man was supposed to treat a woman?

Maybe it's good they're here.

Jalin settled against his sister's shoulder and closed his eyes. She cradled him in her arms, still feigning interest in the television.

Daddy placed Mama's feet back on the ground and kissed her again. "Well, you girls have fun and don't get too loud."

Shanice laughed and punched him on the arm as he wrapped her in a big hug. "You could always join us," she said, knowing full well that he wouldn't. Daddy was not a girl-movie kind of guy.

She kissed him on the cheek as he squeezed her tightly.

"Come here, little man," he said gently, taking the sleepy toddler from Tawny's arms. Her face said she was reluctant to give him up, but she handed him over. Daddy kissed her on the top of the head and said good night.

You want a real man, Tawny? That is a real man.

As Daddy climbed the stairs, the doorbell rang. Mama hurried to answer it.

Tawny tossed a pillow on the floor in front of her. Motioning for Shanice to sit down, she said, "Come on. I'm about to braid that hair."

Shanice sat down on the pillow. She did need her hair redone, and Tawny was masterful when it came to braiding. All the way back to kindergarten, Tawny would braid her hair into neat designs even better than Mama could do.

"You sure this is really your hair?" she teased, her fingers swiftly undoing her braids.

Shanice ran her fingers through her hair as well. Cascading around her shoulders, her locks were soon free from the braids.

Tawny laughed. "Shoot, girl," she said, "you got the nappiest white-girl head I've ever seen."

"Hello?" Shanice replied lightly. "Maybe because I'm not white?"

Tawny threw her arms into the air in celebration. "Yes!" she cried out. "You finally admit it."

Mama returned to the room, Chinese take-out containers in her arms and the first-aid box tucked under her arm. She spread out the feast across the top of the coffee table in front of them. "Looking good," she said happily to her daughter. "Before we even get started, we need to change that bandage."

Shanice squirmed a bit as she stretched out her leg. "Can we start the movie so I have something to focus on then?" she asked.

Mama started the DVD and then laid out the new gauze, peroxide, and towels that she needed to clean the wound in front of her. "They said this was going to hurt," she reminded Shanice apologetically.

Shanice nodded.

Tawny got to work braiding Shanice's hair into cornrows with long braids cascading down her back as the movie started. Closing her eyes, Shanice sighed to herself and tried to recline. There was nothing more relaxing than the feeling of someone working on your hair. Though she was a bit of a tomboy, she loved the feel of new braids.

"Here goes," Mama said, grasping a corner of the tape in between two fingers. In one swift motion, she pulled the entire gauze pad off.

Shanice screamed in pain as the scab from the hole was pulled loose from the rest of the scrape. She jammed a fist into her mouth to keep from whimpering. New signs of blood began to seep from the wound.

"I'm sorry, baby," Mama said as she poured the peroxide liberally over the hole. It bubbled instantly. "Almost done."

Tawny just kept working on her braids, and Shanice attempted to focus on the nice feeling of her hair being pulled taut across her scalp.

Mama rebandaged the area and planted a kiss on her daughter's head. Gathering up the first-aid kit, she carried it back to the bathroom. The pain as Mama had torn off the scab had been almost unbearable. Happily, it subsided almost as quickly as it came. She had to put up with it for only a few more days.

Mama returned and passed her a container of noodles with a pair of chopsticks protruding from it. Daddy was pretty good with chopsticks, but neither of his two girls could use them very well. Nonetheless, they tried every time they ordered Chinese takeout. Darby had tried to teach Shanice the secrets to their use, but the lesson ended in nothing but fits of laughter. Mama often would use the sticks like a spear. It always made for good bonding time if nothing else. In a way,

Shanice never wanted to master the utensils—it would take away part of the fun of movie nights with Mama.

"What else did we get?" Shanice asked, leaning forward to look in the other containers on the floor as Mama opened them.

Tawny pulled on her hair and bopped her in the head with the comb. "Quit moving," she laughed.

"Cashew chicken, sweet and sour pork, vegetables, fried rice," Mama replied, "and moo goo gai pan and egg drop soup."

"Are we starving?" Tawny asked.

Mama laughed.

Shanice smiled. "We always stuff ourselves on movie-and-Chinese-takeout nights. It's all about eating a little bit of everything we like. It's a girl thing around here."

"And it's good the next day," Mama added, spearing a piece of chicken and popping it into her mouth. "Do you like Chinese?"

Tawny made an undecided face. "Y'all sure do a lot of weird things around here."

"Well," Mama replied, "we'll have to get on that mama of yours to start doing more fun stuff. Once you guys get all settled back in, things will be different."

"Things'll never be different," Tawny mumbled in reply.

Shanice looked at Mama. She either didn't hear or chose to ignore what Tawny said, because she didn't respond.

As the movie played and they munched on the Chinese fare, the weight from the past week's events slowly lifted. By the time Tawny was finished with her hair, Shanice was thinking that maybe the summer wasn't going to be as bad as she thought. Even though she and Tawny had had a rocky start, they would do okay together. They weren't going to agree on everything, but to paraphrase Andria, two teens weren't always going to get along in the same house. She needed to be realistic.

"Now go look in the mirror," Tawny instructed.

"Not yet," Shanice argued. The movie was at a pivotal moment in the story. She'd only seen it about fifty times, but she hated missing a minute. "It's getting good."

"Pause it already," Tawny said impatiently.

Mama pushed the button on the remote and examined her daughter approvingly.

Tawny followed Shanice into the half bath. A wide smile covered Tawny's face as she watched her cousin inspect her reflection. She crossed her arms in front of herself. "Now you're looking like a girl," she stated.

Shanice really didn't see much of a difference. The cornrows were straight and tight, but it was nice to have the braids running down her back instead of pushing them out of her face all the time.

"Cuz, you even look black."

Shanice rolled her eyes. "Would you quit that stuff?"

"Quit what?"

"All this black stuff," Shanice replied. "I'm sick of it. Just give it a rest, will you? I'm not black. I'm not white. I'm both and it's okay with me. It needs to be okay with you, too, because neither one of us can change it."

Tawny stared at her for a moment. She licked her lips, obviously trying to think of what to say in return. Suddenly, she took Shanice by the shoulders and turned her around to face the mirror. "Look in there, girl," she said. "What do you see?"

I see what I always see. I see me.

She stared at her reflection, wondering exactly what it was that her cousin was getting at.

"Do you know what your friends see?" Tawny continued to ask questions without giving her the chance to answer. "Do you know what the world sees when they look at you?"

Do I look like I really care?

"I'll tell you what they see," her cousin answered herself. "They see black."

"But I'm only half-black," Shanice proclaimed, tired of the conversation already.

"Cuz, for generations white guys have been making babies like you, and the world still sees them as black. Biracial is still black to most of the world."

Shanice was fuming. Her daddy wasn't some *white guy* who had *made a baby* with a black woman. He was her daddy. His whole world was wrapped up in a black woman and their half-breed baby, and he *loved* them and cared for them. There was no way she was standing silent while her cousin shifted some old social blame on her father. Spinning around to face her cousin, she clenched her teeth and her nose flared angrily. "Don't even go there," she hissed. "Don't you dare go dissing my dad."

"You need to join the real world," Tawny stated as she folded her arms and leaned against the side of the bathroom door. "The rest of us don't live in a color-blind world like you think they do. When people see you, they see black. And when they look at you, they feel sorry for you because you're confused about what you are. I'm not trying to dis anyone. I just want to see you embrace who you are and start acting like it. Quit running around pretending to be some white girl."

Shanice brushed past her as Tawny laughed cynically and headed for the kitchen. "What's that supposed to mean? Are you saying I need to stop skating? Stop listening to rock music and hanging out with my white friends? I embrace who I am, Tawny." She stopped and turned toward her cousin. "I am Shanice Ella Stevenson. I am black. I am white. I like secondhand clothes and music I can mosh to. I think there are white boys who are cute, and I think there are black boys who are cute. I'd much rather bite it on skates and spend the day in the hospital than walk on a basketball court. I choose to be me, not a walking stereotype. I feel sorry for *you* that you're too afraid to do the same thing."

Tawny stared, her eyes burning right through Shanice and into the wall behind her.

Shanice kept her eyes fixed, refusing to back away. She was not going to be the meek little girl who ran to Mama crying when her cousins teased her. That girl didn't exist when they weren't around, and she wasn't going to let her return this time. Her heart beat wildly as she anticipated the backlash she was sure she was about to receive. Tawny could outlast anyone in a battle of wits—Shanice had witnessed it many times before. She was sure she was about to get stomped, but this time she wasn't backing down.

Drawing in long gasps of air, Tawny bit her lip, letting her gaze fall to the floor. Then, without a word, she hurried to the stairs and rushed up to her room.

With a sigh, Shanice slumped against the cabinet behind her. Had she just won?

Mama appeared in the doorway, crossing her arms and ankles as she leaned against the frame.

Shanice scanned her face for some expression of how she felt. *Does Mama feel like Tawny? Mama's black. Does she think I'm deliberately ignoring that part of who I am?* The horror of realizing that maybe she had been disappointing Mama enveloped her. She couldn't bear to think of it.

"Did I do the right thing?" Shanice finally whispered.

Mama crossed the room and pulled out a chair at the table. She sat in the seat beside it and motioned for her daughter to join her. "What's God telling you? Right now, in your heart, what's He saying?"

Shanice sat down in the chair and closed her eyes. All of her thoughts returned to wondering what Mama thought of her. Her own fears and indecision seemed to drown out any possible words of God. "I don't know," she said. "How much did you hear?"

"Enough," she replied.

"Did I do the right thing, Mama?" she asked again, desperate for an answer—desperate to hear the right answer from Mama.

"This is one of those times that I can't answer for you. I just hope I taught you well enough to answer that for yourself."

They sat quietly as Shanice laid her head on the table. She wished she could see what Tawny was doing right now. If she could just know how she was reacting to what was said, then Shanice would know if she had done the right thing or not.

"All I can say," Mama said, rising to her feet after a moment, "is you can't let it end this way if you can help it. This is family. And if you can't change the world starting with your family, you can't change the world—period."

CHAPTER 18

Climbing the stairs quietly, Shanice listened for some sign of her cousin. She hoped to get to her room without running into Tawny, but at the same time, she wished she could talk some more with her. The issue was out in the open now, so why not deal with it and get it over with?

Whoever said, "Sticks and stones may break my bones, but words can never hurt me," must not have been different from everyone else around him, she reasoned. *Because words do hurt. Sometimes they hurt a lot.*

She huffed at herself angrily. Why did she get this way around her family? The Shanice her friends knew wouldn't run to Mama crying when something hurtful was said to her. If she were that fragile, Parker wouldn't have tried to protect her from herself on that first day he and Elijah met Tawny. But being around her cousins—wanting to be one of them while being herself—tongue-tied her every time she was around any of them. Mama talked about family all the time, and deep down, Shanice desperately wanted to feel like an important part of the family Mama treasured.

Well, it isn't happening anymore.

Starting with Tawny, she was going to show them who she was, and if they didn't like it, they were just going to have to deal with it. As she started past Jalin's room, she saw Daddy sitting on the little one's bed. Tawny was standing in a defensive position with her back to the door.

Shanice hurried out of the doorway but couldn't stop herself from lingering close by.

It might not be right to spy, but Shanice had to know what was going on. If Tawny even tried to bad-mouth her daddy, she would set her straight. Pressing herself against the wall outside the room, she strained to hear what was being said.

"He's already got a dad," Tawny was in the middle of saying.

"I know that," Shanice's daddy replied, his voice taking on that gentle tone that she heard him use most often when he was disciplining someone at school. "I don't want to be his daddy. Maybe I could be his favorite uncle, though."

"He's got one of those too. Uncle Raymie is his favorite."

Uncle Raymond was Mama's oldest brother. Shanice had only met him one time in her life. He had stayed on one side of Grandma Leona's house while Mama kept to herself on the other. She remembered Mama refusing to look at her brother across the room. She also remembered Daddy telling her mama to quit being bullheaded and work things out with him. A short time later, Raymond left. Shanice wasn't sure if Mama ever did talk to him. She didn't know what it was all about, but she figured it had something to do with her daddy. Everyone in her family who had a problem with Mama felt that way because of Daddy—and probably their daughter too.

"Well," Daddy replied, not missing a beat, "I'm glad he's got Raymond. He's a good man."

"He don't like you."

Shanice's heart skipped.

There she goes—being all mean again just for the sake of being mean.

"Those are adult things to work out, I suppose, and I hope we can get past them," Daddy continued. "Look, Tawny, I'm not competing with anyone here. We're all family, and I'm just doing my part to help your mama out. I don't have any of my own family left. They're all gone—my parents and my sister too. You guys are all the family I have left now. It's nice to have a little man around the house. It's nice to have both of you here."

"Well, don't get too used to it," she replied. "Mama's going to send for us any day now. And if Jalin is all attached to you, then it's going to be really hard on him to go home."

Daddy was quiet. Shanice desperately wanted to peek back in the room and see his facial expression. Was he sad or just trying to figure out what to say?

"Hopefully he'll want to come visit, and we'll come up and see you guys too," Daddy finally said. "He's going to need all the support he can get."

"He don't need nothing from you. What he needs is some strong black role models, and he's got enough of them."

Shanice heard Daddy get up from the bed, so she scrambled from her hiding place outside the bedroom door and bolted into the bathroom.

"He needs a lot more than that," she could hear Daddy say as he appeared in the bedroom doorway. "Good night, honey."

Shanice snatched up her toothbrush and stuffed it into her mouth.

Tawny closed Jalin's bedroom door without saying a word.

Shanice tried to pretend she was brushing her teeth as she watched her father out of the corner of her eye. He stood in the hallway for a moment, apparently trying to decide what his next move should be. His hand lingered over the doorknob momentarily, and then he dropped it. Shaking his head, he looked toward his daughter and smiled.

Another discussion for another day, his eyes seemed to say.

CHHAPPTERR 119

Shanice knocked a second time on her cousin's bedroom door. The first time there was no reply. She looked again at the clock sitting on the bathroom vanity.

It's not even 9:00 A.M. Where could she have gone at this time of the morning?

Trying the knob, she found the door locked.

"Mama," she called down the steps.

Mama, dressed and looking perfect already, came to the bottom of the stairs. "Yes?"

"Where's Tawny? I don't think she's in her room. She's not answering."

"I drove her down to Angelino's fifteen minutes ago so she could fill out her paperwork. She seemed pretty eager to start working."

Shanice sighed in relief. Her overactive imagination's pictures of Tawny huddled in the streets that had been flashing through her head disappeared.

Maybe it was a good thing Tawny was getting a job. She would be in a neutral place at the pizza shop. It might even be the best place to try to talk to her. Shanice would shower and head over to see her.

"How long is she going to be there?" she called again.

"If you want to have a conversation with me, then you need to come downstairs," her mama replied before walking away. "Civilized people don't shout at one another."

Why does Mama have to be so "Mama" all the time?

Still in her pajama pants and a YMCA T-shirt that she had worn to bed, Shanice headed down the stairs, hopping on one foot as she cradled her crutches in the other hand.

"I need to change that dressing," Mama said. "Come sit down at the table. I made some French toast to ease the pain a bit."

"Just for me?"

Mama smiled. "Yes," she replied, "just for you. Though I hope you'll be willing to share some with Jalin."

"He's too cute not to share with," Shanice said.

"Oh, he sure is," Mama replied. "That boy's got to be the cutest little child in the whole world."

Shanice made her plate and sat down at the table. A thousand thoughts raced through her mind. She wanted to ask Mama if she ever regretted not having black babies. Did she ever wish her only daughter would show the world that she was black? She wanted to know if Mama sometimes wished they were part of a community that looked more like her. Did she ever wish that she and her husband could walk through the mall without someone doing a double take? Did Mama ever regret the decisions she had made?

But then again, Mama might get disappointed in her for even asking such things.

"Here we go," Mama said as she started to change the bandage.

Biting her bottom lip almost to the point of bleeding, Shanice stifled the scream before it escaped her lips. She wasn't going to let herself cry out this time.

The patter of Jalin's little feet across the hardwood floor broke her from her contemplation. Crawling up into the chair beside her, he smiled at Shanice and said hello.

"Hello," she replied before rubbing his head playfully. "He doesn't say much, does he, Mama?"

Mama set a plate of French toast in front of her young nephew. "Let's say our prayers," she instructed him.

After he finished his blessing, Mama turned her attention back to her daughter. "That's what happens when you have babies when there were other issues that you should have dealt with first. Raising children is hard, godly work. When you have to put all your energy into saving yourself, the little ones get the short end of the deal."

Shanice felt terrible. No wonder Tawny was so protective of him. Living her *Brady Bunch* life, Shanice probably hadn't dealt with a fraction of what her little nephew had seen. And he was an angel all the same.

Shanice smiled at him softly as he stuffed a sticky piece of his breakfast into his mouth. Syrup ran down onto his pajama shirt. Mopping it up as best she could with a napkin, Shanice laughed as most of it soaked into his shirt.

"I love my sister," Mama said, loading the dishwasher as she talked. "But I don't agree with the way she lives. God weeps when a marriage ends. Even one as messed up as hers was still blessed by God's grace, and if they would have turned to Him, they could have made it. Unfortunately, Tiesha turned away from Him a long time ago. Some love and attention is what this baby needs. In no time, he'll be caught up to where he should be."

"Did you date black men before you met Daddy?" Shanice tried to suck the words back in before she said them, but it was too late. There they were hanging in the air. Slumping down in her seat, she bit her lip again.

Mama laughed. "Oh, girl," she said, shaking her head, "I met my share of brothers. Some of them no good and others just too good."

Shanice smiled.

"I didn't wake up one morning and decide I was going to fall in love with a Caucasian man, if that's what you're asking."

"That's not what—"

Mama raised a finger to her daughter's lips. "We were both involved in campus ministries at Case Western, and I had known him for a few months before I ever realized I was interested in him. One Saturday, we did a service project in eastside Cleveland, and I saw your daddy playing with these dirty, nasty little kids from the ghetto. When others in our group, including a number of brothers, were too disgusted and hesitant to touch those poor babies, your daddy was picking them up and carrying them around on his shoulders and spinning them around in circles. Everyone else felt sorry for the little guys, but your daddy loved them. And that's when I fell in love with him."

Shanice leaned forward, her chin resting in the palm of her hand. The story wasn't new—she had heard it many times before—but it never grew old to her.

Feeling bold, she asked, "Didn't you worry what people would think about him being white?"

"When I fell in love, I fell hard, and I didn't see a white man. I never even thought about it being a problem until I saw the way my family reacted to him," Mama said as she took a seat at the table and poured Jalin some juice.

"Campus life is a world all its own. Sometimes it's too bad that the real world can't hold on to those same ideals about race, creed, and social issues that so many are passionate about in college. Had more of my siblings been exposed to that, they would see the world differently. But, Shanice, I have never once regretted being with him. God put your father and I together so that you would be born. And I believe in my heart that He's going to use you to move mountains."

Move mountains. . .

Shanice thought of the band. She loved to sing. Second Rate was His vehicle for all of them. Shanice and her friends were going to move mountains *together*.

Mama watched the toddler stuff bites of French toast in his mouth. "Sometimes I wish your daddy hadn't taken that principal job at the middle school here," she said, turning her attention back to her daughter. "I would have liked you to grow up in a more diverse area than this. You and your friends, you don't understand how good you have it here."

Yeah, it's a real utopia. Just ask the twins as their parents scream at one another or Parker as he sneaks out of the house to get to church or Elijah as he sees his mom's name in the paper again for being arrested for drug use. No, we don't know anything about the "real world."

But then again, what had she ever experienced of that world on her own? Nothing. She was the one with the happy home life and parents who were steadfast Christians.

"I couldn't imagine growing up anywhere else," Shanice argued. "I love it here."

"Sometimes I'm afraid that I haven't exposed you to enough of black culture. You get the extremes. You live in a virtually all-white suburb and then you visit your relatives in an all-black neighborhood. The black world isn't all ghettos and violence. All black men are not like your Uncle Antony or my papa was. Too many of them are, but too many of them don't get enough credit for not being like that. And your daddy is not a good guy because he's white."

"Oh, I know, Mama," she replied. She wasn't that blind.

Mama stood up, signaling that the conversation was about over. "And someday, baby," she said, hugging her daughter around the neck, "you'll find the man God intends for you. Black, Caucasian, Asian, Hispanic—I don't care. As long as you feel God's touch on the relationship, I will be happy and supportive of it."

"Y eah!" Parker yelled as the last chords still sounded. "We are going to rock the house tonight!"

Jenna Rose smiled and high-fived Elijah.

Bobbing her head up and down to the beat still fresh in her head, Shanice sighed in contentment. She loved that adrenaline rush following a performance. Even though this was simply the last practice before the show that evening, a small lunch crowd had followed Chance into their practice room and made themselves at home.

The crowd cheered, and some were even on their feet.

Chance walked up front, clapping as he went. He grabbed Jenna Rose's microphone and thanked the audience before mentioning the performance later that night.

"We'd love to see you all out there," Jenna Rose added with a big smile and a bit of southern drawl left from her life in the South.

"Nice touch," Chance whispered as he put the microphone back into its stand. "It's always a plus when the cute blond is the one who invites you out." He waved the whole group around a nearby table. Watching the rest of the patrons file through the door into the dining room, he rubbed his hands together in thought.

"Great job, guys," Parker said.

Chance nodded. "It was very good, guys," he agreed. "You guys have the talent. You have the sound. We just need to work on your stage presence." He turned to Parker and tapped him on the chest. "When the show is over, the first thing you need to do is thank the audience and mention your next show. Always tell them when and where they can see you next. Even in an impromptu show like this, mention it. You got one person out there watching you? You thank him and you tell him where to see you next."

"Yeah, yeah," Andria mumbled, "don't beat a dead horse, Chance. We got it."

"I'm being serious, Andi. You build your following through your shows, and people need to know how to see you perform again. Back to stage presence," he continued, punching his cousin in the arm. "Everyone get back up there with your instruments. We're going to rearrange your placement on stage."

The group hurried back up on stage.

" 'Lijah, you need to stop hiding behind Darby." He pulled Elijah off to one side. "I know you like to be back here by Andi, and that's good since you both make up the rhythm section. But we do need to unbunch you two a bit. If you can stand to be away from her for an hour, I'd appreciate it."

Smiling at his other cousin, who was perched on her bar stool, Chance shook his head and prepared to do battle.

"I will not get rid of my seat," Darby stated, defiance coming through her voice loud and clear.

"It shows your character," he admitted.

"I will not, Chance."

"Okay," he compromised after a moment's thought. "You don't have to get rid of it. But I want to move you away from the corner too. I want to put you against a blank backdrop instead of having you cluttered in front of the drums. Most of our venues are going to be larger than this and we need to be prepared for them."

"Yeah," Andria joked, "move everyone out of the way of the real talent."

"Har, har." Parker stuck out his tongue as he fingerpicked a familiar melody on his guitar.

"I like the way you move around," Chance said to Parker with a grin. "Sometimes it's a little more than the music calls for, but I guess that's what happens when you're ADHD."

Parker stuck out his tongue at their band manager too.

Chance positioned Parker's microphone in front of the drum set. "Kidding. . .just kidding."

He stepped back and looked over the group. "We need Jenna Rose to be front and center." He directed her to pick up her microphone stand and move to the middle of the set. "You always need to be the focus on stage. You are what the people are coming to see."

Wow, I thought they were coming to worship Christ? Shanice smirked and turned her back to their manager.

Just count to three and chill, 'Nice.

"I don't like this layout," Elijah said. "Won't that make us look like a backup band or something?"

Jenna Rose looked around at the others uncomfortably. "I don't want to come across as a solo act. Because I'm not. We're in this together."

"Trust me," Chance said. "Even in a band there has to be a lead singer. The audience wants to know who they are hearing when they see you perform. They don't want to play a guessing game to know who the singer is."

"But we're not about who the singer is," Elijah continued. "No offense, Jenna, because you're awesome. But we're here to worship Christ, not ourselves."

Again, Jenna Rose looked at the others. "I don't want any problem," she said meekly.

"There's no problem, is there, guys?" Chance replied, turning to look at everyone individually. Shanice noticed that each one of them nodded slowly without looking back at him. "We're just trying to make you guys the best you can be. All of you."

Shanice licked the front of her top teeth and avoided his gaze.

Parker nodded in support. "That's why we pay him the big bucks," he said.

"We do?" Darby asked.

"Okay," Parker laughed, "that's why we're *going* to pay him the big bucks someday."

Chance smiled as he stepped back and looked at the group. " 'Nice," he directed, "you need to step back from Jenna Rose and move over to the side a bit. Once again, just trying to space everyone apart."

Shanice followed his directions, moving off to the side and back a few steps.

"Over a bit further."

She moved again.

"Little bit more."

Shanice rolled her eyes and took another small step. *Come on. I'm going to be off the stage by the time you're through.*

Shanice wouldn't have found it surprising. Chance seemed pretty smitten by the blond's natural charms even though he was almost five years older than her. It only took someone about five seconds to see who Jenna Rose's number-one fan seemed to be.

"Shanice and I talk during the show," Jenna Rose pleaded. "I don't want her that far away. We like to be right next to each other."

Yeah, maybe he'll listen to you. . . .

Chance shook his head. "Believe me, half the show is stage presence. There's a certain formula to all this, and to be successful you have to follow it."

"Well," Andria said, catching Shanice's eye, "we tend to stay away from what others consider 'formulaic.' "

"Trust me," her cousin argued. "It'll sound even better having the instruments more uniformly distributed. Plus, this way everyone gets seen by the audience."

Yeah, everyone but me stuck here practically behind the curtain.

"Yeah," Elijah mumbled, plucking the top string defiantly, "but we aren't supposed to be about 'being seen,' are we?"

Shanice looked at him and smiled. No one else reacted to him.

Chance pulled a chair to the back of the room and sat down, leaning forward on the backrest. "Go ahead and play something. Let's hear how it sounds."

They looked around at one another trying to decide what to sing. Finally, Jenna Rose suggested their second song—a song Shanice didn't sing in, just Parker and her. The others agreed.

Feeling completely dejected, Shanice leaned against her microphone stand. First, Chance seemed to want to move her backstage, and then their band decided to "see how they sounded" by rehearsing a song she didn't even sing in. She had never felt quite so invisible as she did right now.

As they finished the song, Chance stood up. "That was great," he said, patting Jenna Rose on the back. "Just great. I think this is going to work. Let's call it a day then until this evening. Get home. Get some rest. And Jenna Rose, take care of that voice. That's what will make or break us."

He turned from the group and exited the room.

Shanice swore she saw dollar signs in his eyes as he left.

CHAPTER 221

Jenna Rose. Jenna Rose. Jenna Rose.

Shanice was starting to feel more and more like her life was just some long, cruel *Brady Bunch* parody with herself starring as Jan Brady. Second Rate was *their* band—not the instrumental sounds of *The Jenna Rose Show*. They had all agreed from day one that no one was more important than anyone else. Each member had agreed that no one would allow this to become all about Jenna Rose, no matter how perfect her voice was.

Yet no one stood up and said anything against the idea to Chance. They all stood by and agreed with everything he said. And of course she couldn't be the one to dispute anything. She would just look like a jealous backup singer and nothing more.

She made her way home a few steps behind the McKennitt twins, pretending like her leg hurt too bad to keep up. Honestly, it felt pretty good—she was debating trying to get back on skates soon.

"Why are we being so quiet?" Andria asked, stopping so Shanice could catch up. Darby continued on.

Shanice sighed and decided it was time to tell her friend the whole story about her cousin and the confrontations they'd had since her arrival. They strolled along from the plaza at a leisurely pace as Shanice talked.

When Shanice was finished, Andria stopped and looked at her. "Well, you know," she said, "she is kinda right. You really don't act black."

"Act black?" What exactly is acting black? If I'm half-black and half-white,

what way am I supposed to act? Act like one part half of the day and the other part the other half of the day? Talk about stereotypical.

"Yeah, whatever," Shanice mumbled in return. She wrinkled her brow, still taken aback by her friend's comment. She picked up her rate of speed and looked straight ahead.

What's your problem, 'Nice? Andi says stuff like that all the time, and you've never gotten upset before. It's called "teasing," dawg. Get over yourself.

This time, however, it stung.

"What's going on?" Andria asked as she hurried to keep up with her friend.

Look at you, Goth girl. You don't like it when people make cracks at you about casting spells all the time.

"How am I supposed to act, Andi?" Shanice stopped and spun to face her friend.

"Geez, I was just playing," Andria responded, backing up a step.

"That's like taking one look at you and thinking you're a witch or something. Don't go playing that stuff with me."

Dumbfounded, Andria's mouth dropped.

Shanice started walking, trying to ignore the slight pain that was building up in her ankle again. As they reached her friends' home, she hurried past without saying good-bye.

"Yeah, okay, bye," Andria called out.

Shanice waved over her shoulder.

I can't believe she actually said something like that.

The house was quiet as she entered. Mama's car wasn't in the driveway. As she scoured the refrigerator for something to eat, she wondered vaguely where Mama, Tawny, and Jalin could have sneaked off to. Just as quickly, she shook off the idea. Did she really care where they went? Just the chance to be at home alone for a bit was welcome. She could actually lie down on her couch, remote in hand, and relax on her own. It felt like forever since she had done that.

Settling on a bowl of grapes, she closed the door and went into the living room. Toys were spread all over the floor. She kicked her way through and found the remote.

Before she could get comfortable on the sofa, the kitchen door banged shut.

No one else gets yelled at for slamming that thing.

Tawny, dressed in jeans and a formfitting shirt that resembled a Detroit Lions jersey, walked in.

Not even ten seconds of peace.

Without saying a word, she plopped down in the recliner. Trying to ignore her, Shanice flipped through the channels, purposely avoiding the video channels that her cousin always watched. Finally, she stopped on a home decorating show. She wasn't really interested in it—she simply hoped it would get rid of her unwanted visitor.

"You going to ask your cousin how her first day on the job was?" Mama asked as she passed through the foyer, the sleeping toddler in her arms. She hurried with him up the stairs without waiting for an answer.

Do I really look like I care?

"How was your day?" she mumbled dutifully.

"It was a pizza shop," Tawny replied, her voice sounding just as thrilled.

"Yeah, well, I gotta rest," Shanice said as she got to her feet. "I have a show tonight."

"You're actually going to go?"

Shanice spun around to face her, surprised. "Of course I'm going to go. I have to."

Tawny picked at a fingernail and twisted her mouth in thought. "That just surprises me, I guess," she said, trying to look bored. "Since they don't even want you there or anything."

Shanice put her hands on her hips. "Excuse me?"

"I might as well tell you since your 'friends' are all too chicken to do it," she sighed. She put her hands down. "They don't want you in that band."

"You're crazy."

"No, I'm serious. I heard them talking right before you got to practice today. They were saying that the best thing that ever happened to them was the Barbie doll, and that they never would have gotten this far with you as the lead singer."

"Jenna Rose has an awesome voice," Shanice mumbled.

This can't be happening.

"Secondary," Tawny said with a dismissive wave of her hand. *"You* have an awesome voice too. She's going to get them farther because she looks like some movie star, and, well, you look like you can't keep yourself clean."

CHAPTER 22

The van's horn sounded a second time outside.

Shanice looked again in the mirror at her reflection.

Dirty? She says I look dirty?

When she was about seven or eight, a boy at school had called her "dirty." Shanice had gone home that night and scrubbed herself until her skin was pink to get herself clean. The next day at school, she bravely walked up to the boy on the playground and announced to him that she wasn't dirty anymore.

The boy and his three friends walked away from her laughing, proclaiming that she was always going to be dirty no matter how much she washed.

That was the first time she had ever faced racism aside from the remarks of her cousins.

Her hazel eyes stared back at her through the mirror. She didn't understand why someone would say such a thing. Her skin was beautiful. While other girls her age were slathering on the makeup to cover acne and uneven skin tones, hers was practically flawless. She looked in the mirror and saw no imperfections at all. She did have a few freckles, but they were minimal and not blotchy to the point that they looked like dirt.

Once again, too light to be black, too dark to be white.

"Shanice," Mama called up the stairs, "your ride is here."

"I'm coming, Mama," she yelled back.

Am I? What would they do if I didn't come down? Would they leave without me or would they come get me? And if I said I couldn't make the show, would they go on without me?

Deep in her heart she was positive that Tawny wasn't telling the truth. She couldn't be. Her friends wouldn't do that to her. They just wouldn't feel that way. Second Rate wasn't about using Jenna Rose to get to superstardom any more than it was about any of them getting anywhere without the group entirely. It was about being together, teaching others about the Bible, and, most importantly, worshiping God. That's what it was all about. Tawny had misunderstood or twisted their words around just to get back at her cousin.

But back at me for what? What did I really do to her that would make her lie to me? And what about Andi's comments today about the way I act? What about the way they're all falling over themselves to please Chance? It's all becoming less and less about worship and more and more about "the image" he wants.

"I just want you to see how other people see you." Wasn't that what Tawny said the other day? Maybe she wasn't the enemy here—maybe her cousin was the one on her side.

Maybe her friends thought she needed to start acting black too—whatever that meant.

She closed the bathroom door and hobbled down the stairs.

Tawny was sprawled out on the sofa. "You're really going?"

"Yes."

"That's sorry."

Shanice hurried through the front door just before Chance honked the horn again. Parker slid open the door as she ran toward the van.

"Where you been?" he asked.

"Busy," she replied, climbing past him and into the seat on the other side of the van.

He pulled the door closed as they backed out of the driveway. A mid-sized pickup with their equipment neatly stored in the truck bed fell in behind the van. Shanice wasn't sure who the driver was.

Jenna Rose turned around in the front seat. "You look great," she said to Shanice.

Shanice looked down at herself and smiled before thanking her. She wore a pair of khakis that flared dramatically at the bottom, sandals, and a flowery, flowing-armed shirt that resembled something from the forgotten realms in the back of her mom's closet. Actually, she probably got it from her mom's closet.

"It's a bit mellow," Andria mumbled from the backseat, still sounding sore from the confrontation they'd had earlier in the day.

"I was having a mellow day, I guess," she snapped back.

"Well, I think you look great," Jenna Rose said.

Great. The Barbie doll likes the way I'm dressed. Shanice winced and mentally chastised herself. *Why am I getting mad at Jenna Rose? What did she do wrong?*

Shanice settled into her seat and looked over at the blond. Jenna Rose looked like a star, just as Shanice had expected she would. Her hair was perfect—the beautiful blond locks flowed around her face and shoulders. She wore a pair of gray flared sweats with white stripes down the sides and a matching jacket that cut off at her midriff. It was short, but the perfect length to just hide skin. The hair, the clothes, and the voice, as always for Jenna Rose Brinley, perfect.

As Chance drove toward their destination, Shanice watched out the window. Her bandmates sang and joked, bouncing the van around as it headed down the road. Parker elbowed her more than once, but she stopped responding to him after the first time. When she turned away from the glass, she caught questioning glances from both twins but didn't feel ready to deal with their concern, so she fixed her gaze on the town passing outside.

How did those lyrics go she had written down the other night?

> *Sometimes I feel kinda hopeless*
> *Sometimes I don't even know why I want to try*
> *Don't you know*
> *Sometimes I feel like giving it all up inside*
> *Sometimes I just want to cry out*
> *For the answers that I seek*

Sometimes I can't take any more of this
(Can't keep it all inside)
I just need to be shown the way
And then it all comes together
When I see Your holy face.

She wished she had her notebook so she could finish the song, but if the others saw it, there were sure to be questions. And right now, she didn't want to answer to any of the others about what she was doing. Besides, if Tawny was right and they didn't want her in the band anymore, they wouldn't need her lyrics.

When I see Your holy face. . .

How long had it been since she'd seen His holy face? Of course, she'd never *really* seen it. Not in the flesh, of course. But when she prayed, when she worshiped, and when she studied her Bible, she'd seen Him plenty of times. That was what the rest of the song needed to convey. She just couldn't work on it now. But she didn't want to lose her thoughts before the show was over and she was home again either.

It's no wonder Darby carries that journal of hers everywhere. You never know when the inspiration is going to hit you.

The van stopped in front of a row of well-designed brick storefronts on the upper side of town. The second shop bore a bright orange sign with neon blue words that said "Plaza Java." White steaming coffee cups were etched on the glass windows, and two wrought-iron table and chair sets surrounded the entrance. A red and white striped canopy flopped lazily in the breeze.

"Cute place," Darby said. She was dressed in her favorite polyester plaid pants and her black "Christian girl" T-shirt. Her clunky black boots were so shiny they sparkled.

The group poured out of the van and into the building. The rich smell of coffee greeted them as they opened the door.

Elijah had on a pair of worn, thin-cut jeans and an old church camp T-shirt, and Parker wore a baggy pair of jeans and a white cowboy-cut shirt with silver snaps down the front and the arms rolled to the elbows.

Like most days, Andria sported her usual cutoffs and white tank top.

Shanice examined the room in front of them. A stage area spanned the back wall with a wooden cross as a backdrop. An eclectic mix of vintage hardwood chairs of various colors surrounded round oak tables. The service bar was the same matching oak finish as the tables and had the usual jars of coffee beans and baked goods standing temptingly within reach. Jutting from the main room, a smaller section of the building housed big overstuffed furniture, a brick fireplace, and walls lined with shelves of books.

Jenna Rose inhaled deeply. "I love that smell," she said.

"Why didn't I ever know about this place?" Darby asked herself as she took in everything.

"Because you would move in," her sister replied.

"The concert doesn't start for another two hours," a friendly man behind the counter said. "You're welcome to hang out until then."

Parker and Shanice looked at each other. With a wink of his eye, Parker turned his attention back to the man. "Thank you, sir," he replied. "Um, we're the band."

With a laugh, the older man came out from behind the counter and introduced himself as Pastor Jimmy. "You kids are getting more and more ambitious and starting younger and younger these days," he said. "Or I'm just getting old. Either way, I apologize." He instructed them to bring the van around to the back of the café so they could unload right onto the stage area.

Double doors were tucked nicely into the side of the stage that led into the alley behind the café. Shanice propped open the doors as the others began to unload and set up the stage.

Tawny's comments kept flooding through her head. Had she actually heard them say they didn't want her in the band? Or did she just conclude that on her own based on what had been said? Shanice needed to find out or she would obsess over it all night.

"Parker," she called as he scrambled from the back of the truck to the stage with a large speaker. "I need to talk to you."

Parker gave her a funny look and hefted the speaker into place.

"Hello? Can it wait?"

Not really.

She found herself nodding instead.

Amber would listen. Shanice followed her friend as she uncovered the soundboard already in place near the back of the room.

"Hey, Amber, I really need to talk to someone."

"Give me about ten minutes," Amber replied, already becoming completely engrossed in her work. She fitted the headphones to her ears. "I need to check out the settings on this thing and make sure everything is okay. Mine's in the van if we need it. Just give me a sec."

She watched her friends from a stool at the bar as they set up their equipment. Amber stood behind the house soundboard, checking out the way it worked. As Parker brought drum pieces in, Andria worked quickly to put them together where they needed to be. Chance was busy wiring the microphones while Elijah hauled in the speakers on a duct-taped dolly with a squeaky wheel.

This really wasn't the time to try to talk to any of them about it. She figured she would just keep it to herself for now, get through the show, and bring it up tomorrow. If her friends didn't think it was in their best interest to have her in the group, they had to know that she would bail out if asked. It didn't make sense to her why they would talk about it behind her back and not just confront her. None of it made any sense, really. Their friendship went deeper than that.

Why am I listening to Tawny?

"Let's get a sound check," Chance called as he pulled up a chair beside Amber.

Shanice jumped up from the bar.

"It's okay, 'Nice," he instructed. "You seem kind of tense right now. Just cool off a bit and get ready. Jenna Rose'll check it for you. She's already up there."

Yeah, sure.

Slumping farther down in her seat, she glared at the back of the college student's head. Who really asked him to be their manager or whatever he was anyway? They'd hired him to take some photos last month, and now he thought he was like their boss or something. Did anyone honestly believe he really knew that much more about the music business than they did? He was majoring in photography, for crying out loud! How did that make him a music industry mogul?

Why are you taking this out on Chance, girl? What did he really do other than put the band first? Are you really so shallow that you are jealous of Jenna Rose? Especially when she's standing up for you?

Yeah, but was she really? Or was it a front?

Sometimes she wished she could just close out that little voice in the back of her head.

People started to make their way in soon after the sound check ended. Second Rate lounged in the cozy room talking about nothing in particular as they watched their audience appear.

"One person or a thousand," Chance stated, "doesn't matter. We do our best."

When did you become part of "we"? Chance's presence was really starting to annoy her today.

The room was packed as the time to go onstage drew closer. Shanice noticed a number of familiar faces from school and church as well as plenty of adults looking for a good weekend show at the local coffeehouse. Regardless of what brought them through the door, they were now interested in getting some entertainment. But she hoped they would get more than that out of it. That's what their ministry was all about, wasn't it?

Parker wrapped his arms around Jenna Rose's shoulders on one side and Shanice's on the other. The rest of the gang gathered around them.

"We gonna tear this place up?" he asked.

Elijah pumped his head in reply. "Oh yeah, oh yeah."

"It's all for You, Jesus," Parker added, closing his eyes and turning his head upward.

"Tear 'em up, Jenna Rose," Chance said as they broke from one another and headed through the crowd.

S hanice could hardly remember much of the show as they boarded the van to return home.

Their spirits were high as they joked and yelled into the night. Parker slammed the door shut and climbed in beside her.

"What a rush!" he said gleefully before elbowing her.

She smiled, unsure of why she didn't feel his enthusiasm. Tawny had passed on their bad news and it was weighing heavier and heavier on her. Something about the whole night reinforced the idea that they didn't want her there. She just didn't get it, though. Could they really not want her around because she wasn't traditional cover-girl material? It was so out of character for her friends.

But they were all pretty smitten by the visions of Chance McKennitt, and he didn't seem above the thought.

Elijah stuck his head out the window and let out a yell into the night air. "We are here, Ohio!" he called out. A car behind them honked. Elijah turned and yelled again. The passenger in the car yelled back enthusiastically. He brought his head back into the van and turned around to the rest of them. "Oh man, I could do this every night."

"I'll call Plaza Java tomorrow," Chance said, "to see if we passed the test to be a regular contributor."

"And we're a hundred and fifty bucks closer to the demo too," Amber said from the backseat. "That regular gig would be sweet. We'll have it in no time. People really wanted to buy a CD tonight, did you see that? People kept asking me what we had for sale. They wanted to buy Second Rate stuff!"

"It's too bad we can't at least get a couple songs or even a single CD done right now," Andria lamented.

"Why can't we?" Parker asked. "You could do that, couldn't you, Amber? Like a live recording kind of thing?"

Amber thought for a moment. "Yeah, we could do that. I'd have to record it and upload it in mp3 form and then burn a few copies. We'd have to get CDs and CD sleeves and covers. It won't be studio quality, but I bet we can do it."

"Having some merchandise would be sweet," Andria added. "That would get us that demo in no time."

"Right now it's all about exposure," Chance said as he pulled in front of Elijah's house. "The more we get your music out there in front of people, the better we get."

"One song has to be one of Darb's," Elijah said before he opened the door. He climbed out and winked at Darby through the window. "Starting tomorrow, we become songwriters."

"I've been writing some songs too," Shanice said quietly. She could hardly believe she'd said the words out loud.

Anything for someone to act like they want me here. . .

"Really? Cool!" Darby replied.

With a big smile, Elijah pointed to Jenna Rose and then Darby as he spoke. "You and you are going to make us stars."

Placing her head against the window, Shanice wanted to crawl into the noisy tailpipe and disappear. *You and you. . .but he said nothing at all about me.*

One by one, the others were dropped off at their homes, until only the McKennitts and Shanice were left.

I can talk to my best friends. . . . Why don't I?

She couldn't bring herself to do it with Chance there. She could feel Andria's eyes on her again, but she wasn't talking.

On the rare occasion of a fight, neither she nor her friend knew what to say. Shanice knew it would end up with them just staring at the other wishing they would know the words to make the fight go away— as if it never happened. The whole friendship seemed much more effective when it was Shanice trying to figure out Andria rather than the other way around.

When they entered the McKennitt driveway, Shanice had her door open before the engine was off. "Shanice," Darby called, "what's wrong?"

"I need to get home," she replied.

She crossed the yard in quick steps as the tears welled in her eyes. Crying was not an option right now. She didn't want them to see her in tears, and she didn't want Tawny to know either. Still, the tears flowed anyway. It seemed the more she tried to fight them, the harder they fell.

"Shanice!" Darby called across the yard.

"I don't feel good, Darb," she lied. "I'll talk to you later. I just want to go to bed."

"You sure?"

"Good night, Darby," she replied as she stepped on the back porch.

Standing by the door for a few minutes, she tried to pull herself together before entering the house. The kitchen was dark, and only the glow of the television flickered from the living room. Daddy was probably already in bed, and if she were lucky, Tawny would already be up in her room too. Mama was probably watching the late-night infomercials she had an unhealthy obsession with. Regardless of where anyone in the house was, Shanice wanted to get rid of any evidence of her tears before she entered.

One last time, she wiped the back of her hand across her eyes, satisfied that she was done.

Tawny, a glass of milk in hand, met her in the kitchen as she entered.

Shanice's heart sank. She gladly would have run into anyone else.

"Hey," Tawny said happily, "did you have a good time?"

"Good night," Shanice mumbled as she locked the door behind her.

"What's the matter? Did they give you the boot?"

"I said, 'Good night.'"

"Don't worry about it. We'll start our own group and just blow them freaks away. We used to have a good time singing, didn't we?"

Shanice kept walking until she was at the foyer, then stopped. "Did you actually hear the group say they didn't want me in the band?"

"What?"

"Who said they didn't want me in the band, Tawny? Did you really hear someone say they were glad that I wasn't the lead singer anymore and that Jenna Rose was?"

Tawny nodded. "They were talking and I heard someone say that the best thing that happened to them was Jenna Rose. They said that everything was coming together now that she was here."

"Tawny, did someone say the words, 'We don't need Shanice'?"

"What's it matter what was said? They said it without saying the words. You have a great voice too, cuz. Why do you think this Barbie doll came along and got your place? Do you think it really had to do with the fact that someone thought she sang better? Her voice is different than yours, but not better. Do you really think she sings better?" She took a sip of milk and shook her head.

"Or is it because she's blond and pretty? Think for a few minutes and you'll know the answer for yourself." She walked back through the room and into the living room. "Night, cuz."

CHAPTER 24

You want to come outside for a bit at least and hang out?" Parker asked. "I know you can't skate yet."

"Nah," Shanice replied through the closed screen door. "I got. . .uh. . .stuff to do right now."

So it went the next two weeks. Days ran together in a blur as Shanice went out of her way to avoid her friends as much as possible. She made herself unavailable when either of the twins or Amber would call. She spent most of her time in her room looking over the songs she had written and wondering if she would ever get the chance to sing them in front of an audience if she left the band. Or if they made her leave.

Three times she went to the pizza shop and went through the motions of practice. When someone asked where she'd been, she would use the "family visitors" excuse. Mama just had her really busy entertaining her cousins. Blah, blah, blah. They all seemed to buy it without too many questions.

Recording the demo singles was heavy on everyone's mind. On the day of the recordings, Chance hurried everyone along. He seemed really edgy about getting the takes done quickly.

"We have to be in the mind frame of being as efficient as possible in recording," he said. "Once we get to use studios, it's not going to be all fun and games. Every second in the studio is money. And for the time being, we don't have much of that to play with."

He hurried them into place without even allowing them to pray.

As Shanice adjusted her microphone, a strange heaviness settled around her. Never once had they done anything without a prayer first. Never. Prayer had always been at the heart of their group—even a big part of their friendship, and they had just discarded it at Chance's request as though it were nothing important. But if no one else said anything about it, did she have the right to?

"Let's try to get this whole song done in one take," Chance instructed. "Knock 'em dead, Jenna."

Shanice looked again at the song list in front of her that had been handwritten by Chance. They started out with an old favorite, "I Could Sing of Your Love Forever," and followed it with "Lift," a worship song Darby had written. "Above All," one of everyone's favorite worship songs, came next, followed by another one of Darby's songs, "Unused."

Shanice hardly sang in "Above All," and "Unused" was the "big" Jenna Rose showcase song. Parker thought that when they performed it live, all of them should leave the stage except Jenna Rose and Darby. It was a beautiful, moving song with an awesome acoustic melody, and Shanice was very proud of her friend for writing it.

With both their version of "I Could Sing of Your Love Forever" and Darby's song "Lift," there was an emphasis on Elijah's rapping flows as well. The sound was cool and all, but once again, Shanice's backup vocals became backup to the backup.

By the time they finished the first song, everyone was all smiles.

Chance pumped his fist excitedly. "That was sweet, guys. Way sweet." He looked again at the sheet. "All right. I know we haven't worked that much on this one, but let's try to get it good the first time." He turned his attention back to Amber. "Can we pull Elijah's flows out a bit more than we practiced it yesterday? And maybe soften Shanice just a bit more? I picture it just a bit more haunting than that."

Haunting? In a worship song? Okay, it might be on the rocking side, and the raps are a bit unconventional. But haunting vocals in a song that says, "Lord, I lift your name in praise; I don't have a thing to offer, but You love me anyway"? Sounds more on the joyous side to me. . . .

But as usual, no one else argued, so why should she?

By the time they were ready to record the last song, Shanice was ready to leave. *Why bother to stay?* she wondered. She didn't even sing in this song, and in the songs in which she did sing, Chance was "softening" her vocals, whatever that meant. Whatever it was, she was certain it would change the way she sounded. He might as well have said that her voice wasn't good enough.

"I need to go," she announced.

Andria stood up from her perch at the drums. "IM me tonight. We'll work on that stuff some more."

Shanice shrugged. "I'll try. I might have family stuff."

Arching her eyebrows, Andria nodded slowly. "Sure, whatever."

Shanice waved over her shoulder without turning around as she exited the tiny practice room.

If anyone seemed to care that she was leaving, they weren't voicing their opposition very loudly.

Shanice found herself spending more time with Tawny than she had expected she would. Not that there was much more for her to do with her sore leg. They hung out watching videos and filling their time with superficial conversations about the performers and their various styles. It was mindless talk, but it filled her thoughts with something other than her failed friendships.

Tawny finally convinced her to spend some time on the courts in the park. Just like Shanice had warned her, the only guys they found were middle schoolers who wished they were gangsters. Actually, it was one of the most fun days they'd had—messing with the wannabes was a good time. The two little runts they played with were totally awestruck at the fact that they had won the attention of high school girls.

She also found herself watching the McKennitt house quite a bit from her bedroom window. Their dad's Mercedes Benz took off in a hurry one day, and she didn't see it return. Darby and Andria were never in sight. If they were such good friends, why weren't they over here knocking down her door to find out what the problem was? It just showed her that Tawny must have been right.

If pressed, Shanice might grudgingly admit the girls had tried to contact her several times, but she convinced herself that they weren't *really* interested in working the problems out. Her fear that Tawny spoke the truth about the band's feelings was simply too strong.

One morning, Shanice woke up to find her mama on the phone. As soon as she walked into the kitchen, she knew something wasn't right. Mama's face was ashen, and the phone hung limply from her hand as she listened to the person on the other side. Shanice sat down at the table in front of Mama and waited for some clue as to what was going on. Daddy, dressed in golfing attire and ready to go, also sat down at the table. Mama reached out and took his hand in hers.

"Okay, baby, okay," mama said, her voice quivery. The sound of it made Shanice's heart flutter. Mama was always the calm one. Mama wasn't supposed to sound scared. Whatever this was, it wasn't good. "I'll be there as soon as I can. We'll take care of things, I promise. I love you."

Mama hung up the phone and laid it on the table in front of her. She placed a hand in front of her mouth and fought back tears as Daddy rubbed her back.

"Let them come, honey," he whispered softly. "There's nothing wrong with tears."

"What's going on, Mama?" Shanice asked. This wasn't good. She hated seeing Mama like this. There had to be something she could do to make it better.

"Where's Tawny?" Mama asked quietly.

"At work."

"I need you to go get her, Shanice. Tell the Angelinos I'm sorry, but I know they'll let her come home."

"I can drive her," Daddy said.

Mama grabbed his hand tighter. "No, I need you to stay. I need to talk to you."

Shanice ran to find her shoes. She stopped in the living room out of sight and tried to listen to what they were talking about.

There was no way she could take off to get her cousin without knowing what it was that was bringing her strong mama to tears. "I could spit nails at her for making me tell her children," said Mama quietly. "But what else can I do? This is my baby sister."

"I know," her husband soothed. "The kids can stay as long as they need to. Tawny will move in with Shanice, and we'll move Tiesha into the office. We'll get her whatever she needs to be comfortable."

Aunt Tiesha's moving in too? What in the world is going on up there in Michigan? And why is it bringing my mama to this?

"I just hope Antony doesn't decide to make things difficult," Mama said disgustedly.

"He has his faults, but I don't think he's a monster," Daddy replied. "He's too selfish to want to take care of his kids. I don't think he's going to give any of us any trouble, whatever is decided."

"I just worry about what's going to happen to those kids," Mama whispered through soft sobs.

"Let's not get ahead of ourselves. We'll do what we have to do for them. We'll take care of them and Tiesha for as long as they need us. Antony is only going to want what's best for them too. We'll get it all worked out. Mama Leona, Raymond, Chaz—we'll get it worked out. Whatever Tiesha decides is best."

Shanice covered her mouth with her hand. Whatever this was, it was bad. They were talking about her cousins as if Aunt Tiesha were gone or something. And they were even talking about Uncle Raymond and Uncle Chaz. Mama never talked about them. Shanice felt extremely guilty for eavesdropping, but this seemed like it was justifiable. In all her life, the only time she had seen Mama this upset was when her papa—her mama's daddy—died. Shanice had been six.

Whatever this was about, it had to be bad too.

"Shanice!" Daddy called.

"I'm coming," she replied.

She scrambled back into the kitchen and hastily decided to take her skates. Her ankle had felt pretty good for awhile, but she hadn't put her feet on wheels since the accident. She knew she'd get to the pizza shop the quickest that way. Slipping her feet inside her skates, she headed into the garage and found her old pair. Tawny had said that she could skate—well, it was time to find out. If nothing else, Shanice would pull her back by her arm if she had to.

"Hey," Andria called from an upstairs window as Shanice went past the McKennitt house.

"No time, Andi," she yelled back.

"Where you going?"

"I need to get Tawny. Family emergency."

"Where is she?" Andria asked.

"At the pizza shop. I've got to get over there."

"I'll call and let them know you're on your way."

Shanice picked up speed as quickly as she could. This was the first time she'd been on skates since she wrecked. For the most part, her scrape had healed well, but the deepest part of her wound was still tender. Her ankle felt pretty normal. She could feel that she still wasn't a hundred percent with every movement, but it felt really good to be skating again.

As she turned the last block before the shop, Mrs. Angelino pulled over in her van. "I got Andria's call and we got Tawny on her way as quick as possible."

Tawny was in the passenger seat. Shanice scrambled in and shut the door behind her, feeling truly thankful that Andria had been by the window at that moment when she passed by.

"I hope everything's okay," Mrs. Angelino said.

"Thank you for the ride," Shanice said. "I don't know what's going on, but I think that prayer would be very much appreciated."

The teens jumped out of the van in front of the Stevensons' house.

"What's going on?" Tawny asked.

Shanice shook her head. "I don't know what it is exactly. Mama told me to come get you right away." She kicked off her skates, leaving them in the middle of the front porch. Mama was sure not to mind this time.

"What's going on?" Tawny asked again as she hurried through the house. Her voice was growing more and more agitated with each question.

She took one look at her aunt sitting at the table, and tears started streaming down her young face. "Where's my mama?" she cried. "He didn't kill her or hurt her, did he?"

Shanice froze as she heard the words escape her cousin's lips. She had never imagined that Tawny's first thought in a crisis such as this might be "Did my daddy kill my mama?" She couldn't imagine how awful that must be.

"Sit down," Daddy said, "both of you."

"Just tell me he didn't hurt her," Tawny pleaded. "Please tell me he didn't hurt her."

Shanice took her cousin's hand as they both sat down. *Lord, I know You're here with us right now. Please let Yourself be known to Tawny. Heal the pain and comfort her. All of us.*

Mama looked at Tawny and drew in a deep breath.

"Oh my God," Tawny wailed. Her cry pleaded with Him to make everything better.

Mama took her niece's hand in hers. "He didn't hurt her, Tawny," she said softly. "Your dad didn't have anything to do with this at all. Honey, after I get done talking to you, I'm going to Detroit to get your mama and bring her back here."

"Why?" The look of relief was soon erased with one of confusion. *Thank You, Lord, that she's not hurt.*

"Tawny, I thought this was something that needed to come from your mama, but you know how she can be sometimes. She couldn't bring herself to do it. She asked me to tell you instead." Mama drew another breath. "Right before you came to stay with us, your mama had a doctor's appointment."

"Yeah, I knew about that," Tawny said, sounding relieved.

"Well, they found that your mama had three lumps under her arm, and they did more tests and discovered that it had spread throughout her body."

"Lumps? Like what? Like cancer?"

Mama nodded slowly. "It's breast cancer. We're bringing your mama back here to stay with us for as long as she needs."

"Until she gets better, right?" Her voice quivered again. "People survive breast cancer, right? That's not a bad one."

Daddy laid a hand on her shoulder.

"She's probably not going to get better," Mama said, the pain thick in her voice. "The cancer is too advanced. When it's not discovered soon enough, cancer can spread to other parts of the body. By the time they found the cancer, it had already spread too far. Uncle James and I will get her all the help we can while she's with us."

Tawny was trembling, but she held fast to Shanice's hand. "And what happens to me and Jalin?"

"We'll come to that as we have to. You will be taken care of, I promise. We'll have to work it all out with your dad and the rest of the family."

Mama got to her feet. "What I need you to do while I'm gone is move into Shanice's room with her. Your mama's going to need the office."

Shanice and Tawny both nodded together.

"When's she getting here?" Tawny asked.

"I'm taking a plane this afternoon to go pick her up. It's a pretty short flight. I got lucky enough to get us back on a plane tonight too. Raymie's meeting me at the airport with her. She says she's really tired, and I would feel better if she wasn't traveling on her own. We have excellent hospitals here in Ohio."

Tawny turned and headed to her room.

Shanice looked at her mama, dumbfounded. Aunt Tiesha was Mama's younger sister. Younger sisters weren't supposed to get terminal illnesses, were they? This kind of thing wasn't supposed to happen in *her* family.

Mama's pain had to be unbearable too.

"I'm going to go see if there's anything I can do to. . ." Shanice wasn't sure what to say. Mama needed someone to lean on, but she had Daddy. Tawny needed someone too.

Daddy nodded.

She followed her cousin upstairs.

Music blared from behind the locked door to the office. Shanice knocked, but there was no response. Leaning against the door, she listened for some sign of her cousin's emotional state. Tawny had just found out her mama was dying. What should her "emotional state" be?

"I know you might not want to talk right now," Shanice said through the door, "but I'm here if you need me. Anytime."

She waited for an answer; when she didn't get one, she walked into the small spare room that was Jalin's for the summer. His tiny frame was stretched out across the mattress, and soft snores were coming from his lips. He was sleeping so peacefully. It was tragic to see his precious innocence as the last bits of his life were unraveling. How unfair it was that this baby had a rotten dad and a dying mother. There was nothing "good" about it. *Why does God allow such things to happen?* Shanice wondered.

At least little Jalin has my mama and daddy—he and Tawny both do.

A sight out in front of the house caught her attention. She crossed the room to get a better look out the window. They were all out there. Parker, Elijah, Amber, the McKennitt twins, and Jenna Rose were holding hands in a circle in front of her home, their heads bowed in prayer.

Part of her wanted to rush out and throw her arms around them, to just bury herself in their love and friendship. But after the past weeks, she was unsure. This was not the time to make a fool of herself. This was not the time to find out that she didn't belong like she wanted.

Sitting on the floor of Jalin's room, she watched them through the window. They stood praying silently for nearly five minutes before raising their heads. Mama and Daddy pulled out of the driveway and waved cordially to the group of kids in their front yard. Andria and Darby both sat in the grass and looked up at Shanice's house.

"I don't know if we should knock or not," Shanice heard Parker say from below.

Jenna Rose rubbed his arm and shook her head. "I think they need some privacy right now. 'Nice will talk to us when she needs us."

Look at them. If they weren't my friends, would they be out there like that?

Jalin rolled over, stretched, and looked at her sitting on the floor beside his bed. A big grin covered his face. "Hi," he said.

"Hello," she said back.

He crawled out of bed and into her lap. His little body snuggled up against her chest, and a sense of peace mixed with sadness enveloped her. She understood now why Tawny grabbed him up whenever she needed security. He was better than the best teddy bear and snuggly blanket combined.

Glancing out the window again at her friends, she wrapped her arms tight around little Jalin. They would have to wait outside. This wasn't about friendship—this was about family.

CHAPTER 26

Shanice placed the last glass in the dishwasher and closed the door. She wiped the surface of the counter with a dishcloth and hung the towel on the oven door handle. Mama had always been adamant about keeping her kitchen spotless. Luckily for her child, that meant she seldom assigned chores that involved cleaning in the kitchen. The kitchen was Mama's domain.

In the week since Aunt Tiesha moved in, Shanice had done more in the kitchen than ever before. Mama was taking every moment she could to care for her sister's needs and to keep her company. Daddy and Shanice stepped forward and took over some of the cooking and most of the cleaning.

Shanice was surprised to find that she actually enjoyed it. Chores kept her focused on something other than the overwhelming feeling of helplessness that surrounded the family now that Aunt Tiesha was with them. The house was different now—it felt more like a hospital.

As she drained the sink, Shanice watched the rain race in streams down the windowpane. The night Mama had returned from the airport it had started to rain. For the whole week, the rain fell—sometimes heavily and other times in light mists. Every day it had rained.

It's as if the sky is crying with us. . . .

Jalin hardly left his mama's side. Instead of moving into the office, she took his room, and he would often sleep beside her in the full-sized bed. Wherever she was, so was he. His sweet little face seemed to make her feel better. She reveled in his attention, and he couldn't be happier.

Tawny, on the other hand, would hardly stay in the same room with her. Shanice felt terrible for both of them every time Tawny would scurry from the room as Aunt Tiesha entered. She couldn't imagine how hard it must be for Aunt Tiesha to see her daughter run from her, and it had to be equally hard on Tawny to know that her mama was not going to be around much longer. Tawny had returned to the office, and the room became her sanctuary; she seldom left it. Music was always blaring.

Mama entered the kitchen carrying the bed tray and her sister's dinner dishes. Most of the meal seemed untouched. She spied the empty sink and smiled. "Thank you for helping. Sorry I didn't get this tray down to you in time. They can just be washed later."

Shanice was surprised. Mama never left dirty dishes in her sink. Things really were different around here now.

Shanice continued to watch the rain run down the window. "Aunt Tiesha loved the porch swing out back," she said, staring into the dark yard. "It's too bad we took it down."

"After the rain stops, maybe we'll have to get her another one. I'm sure she'll enjoy the evenings in the garden. Maybe a hammock too. I'm surprised she never really had much of a garden in any of the places she lived. She was always right at our mama's feet and up to her knees in mud, helping in the garden."

Shanice nodded.

She wanted to ask Mama how she was doing. She wanted to be grown-up and be a support for her, but she got tongue-tied every time she thought about it. Mamas weren't supposed to lean on their kids for help. It was so hard to ask. And part of her was afraid Mama would say that she was sick, too, or something.

"Tiesha starts chemotherapy tomorrow," Mama said. "She's going to be tired, and it will make her very sick. It's a long shot, but she wants to fight it all the way." She brushed the braids away from Shanice's ear. "We're going to have to be there for her more and more as she goes through this part of it. It's going to take a toll on all of us." She turned her attention to the window as well. "You know, maybe you should spend some time with your friends tomorrow. Go skate or something."

"I don't know," she replied. She had barely had any contact with them since their last coffeehouse gig, and they seemed to be keeping their distance too.

"You have another show coming up soon, don't you?"

Shanice shrugged her shoulders. Was it really that important?

"You know what your aunt Tiesha and I have been talking about all this week? We've been talking about Christ. She worries about Tawny and Jalin and if they are going to follow in her footsteps or come to know Him."

"Aunt Ty is a Christian, though, isn't she?" Shanice couldn't imagine any child of Grandma Leona's not being a Christian.

Mama gave her a look. "Think for a minute, Shanice. Ty walked away from her faith years ago. She thought she could live her life on her terms instead of His. She thought she had all the time in the world to live her life the way she wanted it. She figured she'd come back to Him someday, but she also assumed she wasn't harming anyone living like that. Now that she may be facing the end, she's realizing the time she wasted. She prays that you will help show your cousins the way to Christ."

"I don't know about Tawny," Shanice replied. "If she's hoping for some miracle transformation on my part, I don't know if I can do it. Tawny's pretty hardheaded."

Mama reached out and rubbed Shanice's back. "And so are you. There's no question on whether you can do it or not. It's whether He can do it. And you aren't going to find me questioning Him."

Tiesha walked into the kitchen, her son sitting on her foot, his arms wrapped around her calf. Dark circles surrounded her eyes, and her face looked tired. She was taller than Mama and more shapely, and her movements were less confident than Mama's were. That was something that always struck Shanice about the two sisters—Mama had an air of having all the answers while Tiesha seemed to be always searching out the questions. She was dressed casually in a pair of baggy khaki pants with a matching vest pulled over her white shirt.

"Baby," Mama said to her daughter, "go see if you can talk Tonya into going to the salon with us."

Aunt Tiesha smiled weakly at her niece. "Yeah, honey," she added, "we're going to get me some wigs. Fat bald women are not pretty sights."

Shanice smiled nervously and nodded. "Oh, Aunt Ty," she laughed. She took off up the stairs to get her cousin, secretly glad to get away from the conversation.

Tawny was leaving the bathroom as Shanice stepped into the hallway.

"Mama and Aunt Ty are going to the salon," Shanice said. "They want to know if you're coming."

Tawny shook her head. "I think I'll pass."

"Suit yourself."

Tawny grabbed her arm as Shanice turned to go back downstairs. "Don't go frontin' all high and mighty. Don't forget it's not your mama who's dying!"

"Yeah, but don't forget she's not dead yet, and I think she'd like to spend some time with you."

Tawny released her and opened her bedroom door. "Well, I can't."

CCHHAAPPTTEERR 227

Let's go!" Daddy called up the stairs.

"I'm coming!" Shanice yelled back. She looked at her reflection in the mirror one more time.

Why so nervous? Calm down.

Mama was sure to lecture her about her clothing choices. She could hear her now. Mama hated her favorite pair of camouflage pants—especially when she wore her orange flip-flops with them.

A knock sounded at her door. It opened and Darby stuck her head in. "Hey," she said.

"Oh, hey," came her reply as she continued to look at her reflection. It had been weeks since either twin had been in her room. "I wasn't expecting visitors."

"I just wanted to drop this off for you," Darby replied, handing over the yellow Transformer T-shirt. "It's your show to wear it. It'll look sweet with your camos."

Shanice took the shirt, feeling a bit puzzled.

Okay, if they didn't want me in the band like Tawny claims, why would they pass me the shirt?

She pulled it over the white tee she was going to wear and looked again in the mirror. It still didn't look as good on her as it did on the others, but it would work.

"I think you look the best in it," Darby said, plopping herself down on her friend's bed. "It's a good color for you."

"Thanks," Shanice replied uneasily.

Where have you been the past few weeks? I thought you were my friend. I thought you were supposed to be here for me. So what have I done wrong?

The words formed in her head, but she couldn't get them to her lips. They wouldn't come.

"So your whole family's coming down to Plaza Java tonight?" Darby asked.

Shanice nodded. She wasn't particularly happy about it, but Aunt Tiesha was pretty excited about seeing her perform. When the news came that they had won a spot as a regular contributor at the Christian outreach coffeehouse, Mama had even celebrated with them. She was more than happy to bring her sister out to see the show in a comfortable environment like Plaza Java. If Aunt Tiesha would have had to wait until the block party in two weeks, she might not have been strong enough to be outdoors like that after the chemo treatments started.

"That'll be pretty sweet having your family out there when you sing," she added.

"Anyone else's parents coming?" Shanice asked.

"My dad split," Darby replied. "He says that he's going to be doing a lot of business in Toronto, so he took an apartment up there. He says it's just to save on hotel expenses, but who's he kidding? He doesn't pay those anyway. His company does."

"Oh, I'm sorry," Shanice replied, unsure what else to say.

Darby nodded and smiled weakly. "What can we do? Are you riding over with them or with us?" she asked, eager to change the subject.

Shanice shrugged her shoulders as she rummaged through her jewelry box for all her rubber bracelets.

So that explains to an extent where the twins have been lately—dealing with their own stuff.

Darby watched her for a moment, swinging her long legs from the tall bed frame. "You know, 'Nice, this might not be the best time to bring this up, but something's up with you and I wish you'd talk to me about it. You aren't normally like this. You're the last person to ever hold stuff in when something's wrong. Usually you get it out in the open and just deal with it from there. I don't know what happened this time, but I'm still here."

Trying to catch the snicker before it escaped her lips proved to be more difficult than she thought. Instead, it sounded like she coughed as she choked it back. Darby was letting her know she was "still here"? She hadn't been around in weeks. If Shanice had known that her friends needed her, she would have been there for them regardless of the "stuff" going on in her own life.

As she slipped her hands into the bracelets, she caught Darby's eye. Her friend smiled at her and jumped up from the bed. "We ready?" she asked. "You're riding with the rest of the band," she decided as they exited the tiny door. "You've been holed up away from us for too long."

Shanice smiled at the thought. As she passed her cousin's door, she pounded on it. "Let's go!"

"Not going," her cousin replied from inside.

Aunt Tiesha was halfway up the stairs as Shanice started down. "She says she's not coming," Shanice told her.

"I'm about to get her," Aunt Tiesha replied. "Now you get on up outta there," she called as she reached the top step. "If I have to come in there, you're gonna be sorry."

Shanice laughed as they hurried out the front door. The illness might be eating away at her body, but it sure wasn't destroying her aunt's spunk. She was as feisty as always.

"I'll see you guys there," Shanice called to her dad as the girls walked out into the driveway.

"Maybe I should go and talk to Tonya," her dad said as he turned and looked back into the house.

Shanice just shrugged her shoulders as she scurried across the lawn to the waiting minivan.

" 'Bout time," Parker said in his usual greeting as the girls climbed in the back of the van and pulled the door closed. He handed Shanice a CD. "You haven't seen these yet, have you?"

A photo of them all peeking their heads through the van window was on the cover. Shanice smiled as she remembered that day. Chance had captured every quirky, weird moment on film, making them look like some clownish group of kids instead of a serious Christian band. At first Shanice had thought he was nuts. It didn't seem possible to be worship leaders and a bunch of crazy punks at the same time. But as she later looked through the stacks of proofs, she realized that's exactly what they were—crazy punks who happened to like to worship God in their music. With two guys and four girls, it wasn't the most traditionally set up band in the first place. On the inside of the cover there was a full-body picture of them leaning against a wall with the song titles and legal junk appearing above.

Jenna Rose leaned over Shanice's shoulder from the rear seat. "You look a lot better in that shirt than I do," she said. Jenna Rose was wearing the Transformer shirt in the picture. "I've been praying about your aunt and all. If you need anything, let me know."

Shanice nodded, wondering how Jenna Rose knew about her aunt. Then, remembering that Jenna Rose's father was the associate pastor at their church, she smiled in thanks. She held up the CD. "This is sweet."

"It sounds really good too," Andria added.

Amber tossed her head in disagreement. "Sounds all right for the equipment we have. Good enough for a five-buck price tag."

This time as they neared the coffee shop, they pulled straight into the back and unloaded their gear.

The stage went together in no time as they set up their equipment. Shanice commandeered two tables up front for her family and shooed visitors away as they began to file in and find seats.

By the time the show was to start, the coffeehouse was more full than before—save for the two tables up front. Shanice scoured the crowd as they took to the stage, expecting to see her family somewhere else in the audience, but they were nowhere in sight. As the rest of the band tuned up, she borrowed Jenna Rose's wireless phone and called home. There was no answer.

They must be on their way. She kept trying to reassure herself as Chance jumped on the stage and introduced them.

As she sang, Shanice studied the crowd over and over again, looking for any sign of them. Daddy knew where the coffeehouse was—he had given them the directions in the first place. A terrible feeling was welling in her gut, and by the intermission, it had made its way into her throat.

On their break, she borrowed Jenna Rose's phone again and went outside.

"You guys are fantastic," a voice said as she dialed the number.

She smiled and thanked the teen as he remained standing there, looking at her in awe.

Again, there was no answer on the phone. Making her way back into the building, she fought her way through the crowd to the counter. A young girl grinned widely and asked what she could do for her. "You didn't happen to see a tall white guy with a short black lady and some other black folks, did you?" The room was mostly full of white people, so Shanice figured that a couple black women and kids would be somewhat noticeable—especially if one of them was cozying up to a white guy.

The girl shook her head.

"If you do, that's my folks," she instructed the worker. "Please tell them I've saved seats in the front and to get up there. I don't know if they're here or not."

"Well, you guys are hot," the girl said, looking around appreciatively. "We've never had a crowd like this for any of the other bands we have in. If I see your folks, I'll let them know."

Shanice scanned the crowd again and decided to call one more time. As she made her way back outside, the same young man who had complimented her earlier held open the door for her. He held up one of the CDs. "I would love an autograph," he said.

"I'm sorry, but I just can't right now," she said honestly.

The phone again came up with the answering machine. Shanice looked at the pimply-faced teen, not being able to shake that feeling of dread. "Did you drive?" she asked him.

"Yeah," he replied enthusiastically, "That's my Accord right over there." He pointed to a late-model silver Honda with a raised spoiler and nice rims.

"I have a bit of an emergency. I know the show isn't over, but I have to get home right now. Can I get a ride?"

The boy quickly stood up straight and threw back his shoulders. "Are you serious? Me?"

Shanice was sure he could see her blushing, even with her darker skin and the dusk. Having a guy give her this sort of attention was new. Had the circumstances been different, she might have reveled in it more. "If you can't do it, I understand. I just really need to get home."

"No, no. I'm your man," he said, leading her to his vehicle. Instead of the silver Honda, he led her to an older, sporty-looking sedan with dents and rust spots. "Okay, so that wasn't my car," he admitted. "I didn't think I would actually be taking you for a ride right now." He looked pretty embarrassed.

Confused by his admission, Shanice climbed in and turned her thoughts back to home and especially her aunt. If anything happened to her while Shanice was out playing around, she'd never forgive herself.

As the boy took the driver's seat and pulled his seat belt around his waist, he introduced himself as Jeremy and started the car. Shanice realized that she had never told the others she was leaving, and also that she still had Jenna Rose's phone.

A wooden A-frame placard in front of the building had the coffeehouse phone number on it. Shanice quickly dialed the number as Jeremy headed back through town. "Hello, I need one of the band members," she said into the phone as the girl answered it.

"They're about to go back on," she replied.

"Yes, but I need to talk to someone from the band. This is an emergency."

"Can I take a message and have someone call you back after the show?"

"No, please give me someone now."

The phone went dead.

Well, if I wasn't out of the band before, I probably am now. I can't just run away in the middle of a show and expect everyone to understand and say it's okay.

"You guys are really great," Jeremy went on and on as he drove, talking nonstop about how much he enjoyed Second Rate's music.

Shanice felt guilty for not really paying attention to him. She just hoped she wasn't overreacting. She could imagine Daddy's response right now if the family really did show up and the rest of the band was getting back onstage and Shanice was missing. Poor Jeremy here would be dead meat. Daddy would snap him in half and then ask questions later. It had been one grand adventure after another spending three years in middle school with Daddy as the principal.

"I've been to all of your shows," he continued.

Shanice pointed to her house as he pulled into the drive. Mama's car was missing from the driveway.

"It'd be great to see you again," Jeremy said as she opened the door.

"We play at the eastside block party in two weeks," she replied. "I'll see you there?"

"Oh, of course!"

Yeah, that's the way to pick up a guy.

The back door was locked, so Shanice went into the garage to retrieve the spare key hidden inside a stack of terra cotta pots. She let herself in and called for someone to answer.

No one was home.

She rushed back out the door, hoping to see her new friend still in the driveway. He was sure to get her back to the coffeehouse if she asked. Asking him to take her to the hospital might be jumping the gun a bit—even though she wasn't sure where else they could be.

But he was already gone.

She found the phone book and the telephone. Looking up Plaza Java's number, she dialed and sat down at the kitchen table. It rang a couple times before the girl answered. There was plenty of noise on the other side. "Hello?" Shanice called. "Can I leave a message for the band?"

"The band just packed up and left," was the reply. "One of the members took off, so they didn't finish their set."

Her heart fell to her feet. She was so out of the band now. They were so mad that they didn't finish the show! And now what were they doing? Probably coming to get Jenna Rose's phone and tell her that she was officially done with Second Rate.

She jumped as the phone rang in her hand.

"Hello?"

Mama's voice was on the other side. "Hi, honey. Is the show over already?"

"Where are you guys? I left the gig when you didn't show up."

"I figured I would be leaving a message for you. You shouldn't have left your show! We were on our way when your Aunt Ty passed out in the driveway. We're in the hospital right now."

Shanice gasped at Mama's words. "Is she okay?"

"She's probably going to stay overnight for observation. Daddy and Jalin are on their way home. I'll see you tomorrow, honey. I'm staying here with your aunt. I think we're going to get you a phone soon. With the situation the way it is around here right now, it'd probably be the best idea."

"Is Tawny staying too?"

"Tawny didn't come with us. She's still home. Well, I need to get back. You try to talk to her a bit, please."

Shanice hung up the phone and called for her cousin again. There was no answer.

CHAAPTERR 228

urrying up the stairs, Shanice was surprised to find the office door open. She stepped inside for the first time since the day she had tried to get online over a month before. A clown fish swam through the aquarium screensaver on the computer, and a stack of library books covered the desk. Other than that, the room looked pretty much as Daddy had left it.

Shanice was puzzled at the stack of books. Books on animals of the coral reef, dolphins, and some teen fiction. Who knew Tawny even liked to read—much less be so into this ocean stuff?

She never even knew her cousin had been going to the library. Maybe there was more to her than that urban front after all.

There was no sign of Tawny or where she could be. The library closed at eight, and it was going on nine o'clock.

Shanice checked all the upstairs rooms and bounded back down the stairs. She went through the downstairs again, thinking that maybe her cousin just wouldn't answer her.

She's outside somewhere.

Opening the front door, Shanice called into the night air for her cousin. No reply.

Even though Tawny was the same age as Shanice, she couldn't fight the worry that was slowly taking over her emotions. Tawny had hardly ventured outside in the time she had been there, and if she had taken off for a walk or something, there was no telling how lost she could get. And Tawny was such a live wire that Shanice was afraid of what she might be doing if she was out there. Tawny might just be the type who would run off with some thirty-five year old she had met online.

The computer. . .

Maybe she could find some clue as to where she would be in her files.

She ran back upstairs to the computer and pulled up the Internet, looking for any clue of where she could be. Tawny had a Detroit chat site saved to her files as well as a bunch of music sites. Again, Shanice was surprised to see that the history log was full of sites like *Discovery Channel Online* and *The History Channel.* There seemed to be a lot about Tawny that she didn't know.

The instant messenger she used had one friend online. Shanice sat down and IM'd the friend.

"Sup?" she typed. *"I'm looking for Tawny."*

"How r u?" came the reply.

"U know anything about where Tawny could go? She's not here and I'm pretty worried about her. She's supposed to be here."

"Nah, Tawn's not home right now. She's at this lame cousin's house or something."

"I'd be the lame cousin. She give u any clue where she might go while she's here? This is really important."

"She talked about hopping a Greyhound."

"2 where? Detroit?"

"Yeah."

Shanice drew in a quick breath as she stared at the words. Would Tawny really do something like that? With her mama and brother here, would she try to go back to Detroit? What would still be back there for her?

Her daddy. Maybe that's why she wanted the job at Angelino's.

Shanice signed off the computer without saying good-bye and surveyed the room for any signs of packing. Everything seemed to be in place. No clothes seemed to be missing from the hangers in the closet, and Tawny's suitcase was stuffed under the bed.

Where's the closest bus station anyway?

With a heavy sigh, she hurried downstairs and grabbed the phone book again. She didn't even know where the nearest Greyhound bus terminal was, but she had a funny feeling that her cousin was heading there. If she were heading back to her dad, she would probably have clothes and stuff at his place, so she wouldn't need to pack anything. Plus, if she felt this was her best chance to get out what with being left home alone like that, she probably wouldn't take the time to pack anything.

As she walked through the kitchen, she saw Parker and Andria sitting on her back porch.

Great. Here goes.

She opened the door and stepped outside, finding selfish satisfaction in the echoing sound of the screen door slamming behind her.

Parker's hands were stuffed in the back pockets of his baggy jeans. "Hey," he said sadly.

"I don't have time right now, guys," Shanice said hurriedly. "I'll explain in due time, and I'm sorry I took off like that, but right now I have to find Tawny. She's gone and I don't have a clue where to find her. I have a scary feeling that she's running away—going back home to Detroit."

Her two friends turned and looked at each other.

"We know where she's at," Andria said.

Shanice froze as relief flowed through her.

Parker motioned her to follow him through the backyard. In the moonlight, Shanice made out multiple shapes sitting on the trampoline in the McKennitt yard. She hoped—but would be shocked if—Tawny was among them.

"We came home to find out why you took off. I knew it had to be bad. The band means so much to you and all," Andria explained, "and we found her on our trampoline. . .and, well, she was upset."

Tawny smiled weakly at her cousin as she drew closer. "I noticed that you guys used this as a thinking place. I didn't mean to intrude. I just couldn't stand being in my room anymore." Her voice became flat as she lowered her head. "I don't know. I wanted to imagine how it felt to belong or something."

Shanice shook her head in confusion as Jenna Rose reached over and put an arm around Tawny's shoulders. Shanice pulled herself up beside her cousin. "Mama called. They're keeping your mama overnight for observations, but she's going to be okay."

Tawny dropped back on the rubber mat and stared into the sky. "But she's not going to be okay," she said, her voice barely audible. "She's going to die."

Each of the friends lay down as well, their heads forming a small circle in the middle of the trampoline.

"But not yet," Jenna Rose said, grasping the girl's hand.

Tawny laughed softly and shook her head in disbelief. "But you don't know what it's like to look at your mama and know that she is— that she's going to be gone soon. And there's nothing I can do about it. All that I have and know will be done when she goes. Talk to me when you know about that, okay?"

Shanice stretched her neck to see her friend's face. Jenna Rose was staring into the sky, her face very still and wet with tears. Reaching over her head, Shanice rubbed the side of the girl's cheek in support.

"Actually," Jenna Rose replied, "I do. My mom fought breast cancer for a long time. A long time. She was diagnosed when I was seven, and I watched for almost five years as she got sick, got better, and got sick again. I saw her through the radiation stuff, a couple different rounds of chemo, and homeopathic treatments too. They thought she beat it once. But it came back. She fought until the end, but it took her when I was twelve. So I hate to tell you that I know. . .but I know."

The air was quiet as they digested what Jenna Rose had said. For the months that they had known her, she had never once before said so much about her mother. The twins and Shanice had talked about it, figuring that she must have died, but it was still terrible to know that their conclusion was true.

"My mom is an addict," Elijah said quietly, breaking the silence after a few minutes. "She doesn't have cancer, but she has an illness that will likely kill her in the end too. I've lived with my aunt and uncle since I was eight. I love my mom, but I can't stand to be around her. The drugs have eaten her up so badly that she's hardly anything more than a walking corpse. I pray so hard for her every day that it won't take her. But I know in my heart that it already has. Even if she would get clean, her body's so messed up from it that she'll die from something because of it. So even though it might be a bit different, I know."

"So why won't God make her stop?" Tawny demanded. "You guys are all into the 'God stuff.' Why did God have to take your mom and now mine? Why does God go around doing this stuff?"

"I asked Him that over and over for the past three years," Jenna Rose answered. "And I never got an answer. I hated Him. I didn't want to believe in Him anymore, but I couldn't. I couldn't stop believing in Him, even though I wanted to."

" 'Because if it's Your will, nothing will change it,' " Parker sang softly from a verse out of one of the group's favorite songs.

Jenna Rose nodded. "I still struggle with wanting answers, but it's not our place to demand them. We just have to have faith that He knows what He's doing. And that He'll never forsake us. When I was asking questions, I was a mess, but when I accepted that He was my Savior, I found peace in knowing that He's in control."

"We can't always understand," Elijah added, "but we can have faith that He's always there."

"Your mama has come back to Christ," Shanice shared with her cousin. "My mama says they've been reading the Bible together and praying a lot. Aunt Tiesha wants to know that you're saved too. When she does go, she's going to be with Jesus. No pain. No sorrow. Just an eternity of joy. That's got to be comforting, isn't it?"

In some sense Shanice was asking more for herself. It wasn't her own mother, but Tiesha was her aunt—someone she cared for. And Shanice was finding it very difficult to come to terms with the grief.

Tawny shrugged, still staring up into the air. "If you go believing that stuff, it would be."

"You hang out with us long enough and you're bound to," Parker said as he grabbed first Shanice's hand and then Tawny's.

Shanice took Andria's hand beside her.

"Lord Almighty," Parker called out into the night air, "You alone are the Maker of the universe. You alone are worthy of our praise. You alone know the purposes of each and every one of us. Bless this circle of friends, Jesus. Come among us and help us to comfort one another and be there for one another as only a friend in Christ can do. Lord God, we love You and we lift our joys and our sorrows before You, praising only You. In Jesus' precious name."

"Amen," they all said together.

Shanice smiled, turning her gaze back to the sky. Tawny had even spoken the "amen." It was a start.

Tawny sat up slightly and smiled at her cousin, still holding on to Parker's hand.

A real smile.

And with the smile, Shanice sensed that maybe, just maybe, the old Tawny had returned.

"I might have underestimated your friends," she said.

Shanice nodded. "They are pretty cool people."

Tawny tugged on Parker's hand playfully. "Yeah, not too bad for a bunch of whiteys." She winked at her cousin.

Shaking her head, Shanice sighed and then smiled. "You are sorry."

"Not as sorry as you."

Her Tawny was back.

"You know," Tawny said, "your dad and I had a talk this afternoon before they left." She giggled slightly to herself. "I want so badly not to like him. I really do."

"Wait a minute. . . ," Shanice began to argue.

Her cousin held up a hand. "Hold up. Uncle Raymie, Daddy, Uncle Chaz—they never really talk bad about him. You know, I don't think they really have a problem with him. I just think they don't ever want to give him a real chance. Your daddy seems like he should be boring and stuffy or something. But he ain't."

Shanice smiled warmly. Her daddy was anything but boring.

"I think they feel like he took Aunt 'Nay away. She went to college a poor black ghetto girl and came home a different person. I think Uncle Chaz is scared of her now. Uncle Raymie can't say her name without saying something spiteful about her forgetting where she came from. All in all, I think they're proud of her. I know my mama is." She crossed her legs over the edge of the trampoline and leaned back on her hands. "But, 'Nice, your mama hasn't forgotten anything."

"She's the strongest woman I know," Shanice added.

"She scares me," Elijah admitted.

They all laughed as Tawny nodded in agreement. "Yeah, there are times she scares me too. My mama talks a good game, but she's so weak. With all the stuff Daddy has put her through, she still goes right back to him."

"She probably hopes she can change him," Darby said.

"I don't think so. I think she's too afraid of being without him. She doesn't know how to be without him. But Aunt 'Nay, she's strong like I want to be. Strong in what she believes in and what she wants. It's all in her actions, you know. My mama's so defeated, she's just talked the talk for years now."

Shanice could see her aunt and uncle's marriage being about staying together because of fear of being separate. That's what she thought was the case with the twins' parents—they'd been together so long, they couldn't imagine being apart.

"Anyway," Tawny continued, "your dad came in to talk to me, and man, I wanted him to dis my dad so badly. I wanted him to say something bad about my dad so badly, just so I had a reason to hate your dad. I know what he must think of my dad: an unemployed crackhead, a grown man hanging out on the street corners with pushers half his age." The malice in her voice grew thick. "I wanted him so bad to do it, but he never did." She paused for a moment, seemingly trying to pull herself together. "He's just cool, I guess."

Shanice smiled. "Yeah, he is, for a white guy."

Her eyes sparkled with tears as Tawny laughed lightly. "Yeah, for a white guy."

"I happen to be a white guy, and I think I'm rather cool," Parker piped up, trying to sound offended.

"You're just a dork," Shanice replied.

"Hey, you don't have a bum leg no more, so don't try me."

Shanice stuck a fist in the air and Parker cowered behind Tawny's shoulder, yipping like a hurt puppy.

The stars sparkled in the night sky above them. Shanice watched as they dipped and played behind two misty-thin clouds drifting across the horizon. Somewhere in the distance—maybe at her house or beyond, a car door closed. Daddy and Jalin might be home.

She thought of Mama trying to sleep in one of those recliner chairs at the hospital. Mama was probably hovering over her baby sister who was bigger than she, probably getting in the way of the nurses who just weren't doing things the right way in Mama's eyes. Mama, the strongest woman she knew, was reduced to helplessness as she watched one of her family get weak and face death. It was her mama who still preached the importance of family even though her two brothers hadn't spoken to her in years.

And then the realization of what Tawny had said sunk in. Mama's siblings didn't hate her because she wasn't black enough. None of it had anything to do with her. They just felt they didn't know how to relate to Mama anymore. And instead of talking it out, they—Mama included—were letting all the insecurities and unsaid feelings settle into the next generation.

It has to end here. We are family, and family is what is supposed to be there for you no matter what.

Shanice also recognized that for weeks she had been stressing over information garnered from "he said/she said." This secondhand information, which she always felt in her heart couldn't be true, brought bad communication and mistrust into her circle of friends. Shanice saw that she was making the same mistakes that her mama was making in communicating with the family. She had ignored her friends' efforts to help her in the preceding weeks—all because of her insecurities and unwillingness to open up to them.

"I'm sorry I've been so. . .rude. A brat, I guess, lately," Shanice said to the group after a few minutes of silence.

"You sure have." Parker grinned.

Darby buried an elbow in his side.

"Ouch," he whined. "Remind me not to mess with this girl. She hurts when she plays."

"Seriously, though," Shanice continued, "I pushed you guys away, not trusting you—or even God really—with the stuff going on in my head. And the only result has been feeling more and more alone. It's like a pit, you know, that you dig for yourself. I am really sorry."

"It's okay, 'Nice," Jenna Rose said, breaking her silence. She turned and faced Tawny. "I hope both of you realize now that you don't have to go through this by yourself. I know I'm here for you, and I'm sure the rest of us will agree. Even if you didn't think we'd understand, we are still here for you in whatever way we can be."

The others nodded.

"I wish you would have told us sooner," Darby agreed. "I feel so bad that you guys were facing this all alone."

"Thanks," Tawny sobbed, trying to collect herself. She had begun crying as Jenna Rose spoke.

Shanice dropped her eyes to her feet. "I don't know. Things just didn't seem right."

"That's because you were being a brat," Parker said with a smile.

Darby elbowed him again.

"What? She said it first," he protested.

"Sometimes you need to learn when to crack a joke and when to be serious," Darby scolded him.

"Oh, 'Nice knows that I love her," Parker said.

With a sheepish smile, Shanice buried her face in her hand and rubbed her eyes. Of course, he was right. She knew that he loved her—like a big brother or a best friend. They all loved her. Just like she loved them. Why she had let little seeds of doubt grow so rampant, she didn't know. She didn't even care anymore what Tawny might have *thought* she heard.

The people sitting on the trampoline around her were more than friends. There were times she couldn't fully relate to them, and maybe there were times they couldn't relate to her either. And maybe Tawny fit in better than either one of them wanted to believe. They were different— all of them. Maybe the only thing that should matter was caring for one another and fully believing in a God big enough to bridge the differences.

Maybe different was good—just like she'd always suspected.

Shanice lifted Andria's and Tawny's hands to the heavens. The rest of the group followed suit.

"Friends forever!" they yelled into the night sky, lapsing into fits of irrepressible laughter at their own cheesiness.

Also in the On Tour Series

the perfect girl

Jenna Rose Brinley has the voice of a star—and the looks to go with it. But when Jenna's pop star attitude overshadows her talent, the band wonders: Can she really lead a group devoted to singing about God when she seems devoted only to herself?

From *The Perfect Girl*. . .

Every anticipated memory for the coming months fizzled like an old match the minute Jenna Rose Brinley opened her mouth and that first note sprang forth. A glimmer brighter than the gold tones behind the pulpit appeared in the pastor's eyes, and the youth pastor could hardly contain his glee as he bit his lip. For a brief moment, even Cheryl, the organist, paused and scanned the crowd for the melodic source. One by one, members of the congregation faded away until the only voice left was that of the fifteen year old with the blond locks of hair wisping around her shoulders.

"Who's that?" Andria whispered to her twin sister as she surveyed the new face across from them. The girl, all alone in the second pew, continued with her song as if every voice was still in sync with hers.

Darby gave a fleeting glance. "No idea. Whoever she is, she can sing, that's for sure."

"Doesn't she realize that no one else is singing?" Andria mumbled as she glanced around the sanctuary. Pairs of eyes from all angles of the room were fixed on the young guest.

"I would say chances are she likes it that way."

Now Available in Bookstores

For more info about the band, sneak peeks of upcoming books, notes from the author, and more, check out www.ontourfanclub.com!